PUMPKIN SPICE SCARE

BOOK FOUR IN THE CUPCAKE CRIMES SERIES

MOLLY MAPLE

D1707561

MARY E. TWOMEY, LLC

PUMPKIN SPICE SCARE

Book Four in the Cupcake Crimes Series

By

Molly Maple

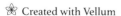 Created with Vellum

DEDICATION

To Winter Wonderland Peanut Butter

My kitten who snuggled me through the duration of writing this book.

(Which is why it took so long to write)

ABOUT PUMPKIN SPICE SCARE

When mischief and mayhem are targeting the staff where Charlotte works, everyone is a suspect.

After Charlotte McKay stumbles upon her coworker's body, theories about who could be targeting the staff at Bill's Diner take on a life of their own. When secret shames are brought to light, it seems anyone could be a suspect in the small town of Sweetwater Falls.

Grudges run high and suspicions even higher when the killer strikes a second time. Forget about finding the criminal— Charlotte is concentrating on making sure she isn't next on the murderer's hit list.

Join Charlotte as she makes new friends and determined enemies in the cozy town of Sweetwater Falls.

"Pumpkin Spice Scare" is filled with layered clues and cozy moments, written by Molly Maple, which is a pen name for a USA Today bestselling author.

1

LAST DAY

*M*y stomach is in knots. I didn't sleep well last night, though I'm not sure how well one is supposed to sleep in situations like this. I'm not a quitter, but today, that's exactly what I'm about to do.

When a knock sounds on my bedroom door, I finish pinning up my blonde waves. "Come on in, Aunt Winnie."

My sweet ninety-one-year-old great-aunt comes in, tiptoeing like she's trying to sneak into the room. "Charlotte, are you coming down to breakfast soon? I've got a surprise for you, and I'm no good with patience. It's the one virtue that never made much sense to me."

"A surprise?" I light up like a little girl on Christmas morning. "You didn't have to make a big fuss."

Aunt Winnie puts her hands on her hips, her silver curls swooshing across her shoulder. "Young lady, it's not every day a person quits their job because their passion project turned into actual income. This deserves a celebration." True joy dances in her glassy sea-green eyes. She looks about ten seconds away from pulling out a camera so she can capture baby's first time quitting a job.

I grimace when I hear something crashing downstairs. "Was that part of the surprise?"

"It better not be. Those girls, I swear..." She marches out of my bedroom, leaving me to finish getting ready for my big conversation with my boss at Bill's Diner, in which I will inform him that I am quitting.

I hustle down the steps, nearly falling on my backside when the kitchen erupts with a joyous "Congratulations!"

How Agnes, Karen, Marianne and Fisher managed to stay so quiet that I didn't hear them come inside this morning is beyond me. In the next breath, I am scooped into hugs and cheek pinches as my closest friends in Sweetwater Falls make my celebration their own. The kitchen smells like ham, which makes my mouth water. I can tell Fisher was in charge of the food because it smells like pure love.

I adore these people. I can't get enough of this precious small town. Moving here from a big city a few months ago was the best decision I've ever made—other than opening a cupcake bakery out of Aunt Winnie's house.

I really didn't see that taking off, but after one short month, I have enough saved to be able to quit my day job and pursue baking cupcakes full-time. Or, I will in two weeks, which is why this morning I am putting in my two-week notice with Bill.

There goes that stomachache again. I don't want to let Bill down, but I think it's obvious that waitressing at his greasy spoon diner isn't my life's calling.

My best friend loops her arm through mine, her grin a mile wide. "I'm so excited for you! I barely slept last night. Are you beaming?" Marianne flips one of her two brown braids over her shoulder, motioning for me to sit at the round table in the corner of the kitchen.

"You know that feeling you get right before you go over the

edge of a roller coaster's big hill?" I motion to my stomach. "That's what I'm feeling. Happy and nauseous."

Fisher slides a plate of food onto the table while Marianne pulls out my chair for me. Fisher grins at my wide eyes as he pushes his black curls away from his round face. "What, you've never seen eggs benedict with country ham before?"

"Not in this kitchen, no. You didn't have to go to all this trouble. I know you're busy at The Snuggle Inn."

Fisher waves off my concern. His hairy forearms are thick. They flex as he sets down silverware beside my plate. "And miss this? Nah. This is a big deal, Charlotte. You've been putting in a heap full of hours, working your day job plus trying to get your cupcake empire off the ground. I only wish I could be there when you tell old Bill you won't be his waitress anymore. He's been getting on my last nerve lately."

"Being his usual charming self?" I tease. My boss is the definition of grumpy.

"You know it." Fisher turns off the stove and slaps my hand. "I have to get back to work. Congratulations, Charlotte McKay. I want every detail of how sour Bill's face looks when you tell him his favorite waitress is quitting." He moves his fingers through his black curls. He's a good decade and a half older than I am, but when he is at work in a kitchen, he looks far younger.

My nose crinkles. "I'm hardly his favorite. Bill can't stand me." The feeling is mutual.

"Aw, that's just Bill's way. Good luck, kiddo." Fisher hugs Aunt Winnie on his way out, leaving me with the best breakfast in the world. Fisher's passion for food matches my obsession with cupcakes, so we understand each other well. Each bite of this meal is a treat. The fact that it was made just for me? I don't know how I got to be so spoiled.

Karen pours herself a glass of orange juice and sits across from me with a half-eaten plate of the delicious breakfast. "No more talk of Bill. It's time for presents!" She surprises me by pulling out a long white envelope and slapping it on the table. "It's from the Live Forever Club."

I glance up at Karen, Agnes and Aunt Winifred, wondering if there has ever been a more fantastic and adventurous group of women. "A present? You didn't have to do that."

Agnes tugs a second envelope from her pocket and sets it in front of Marianne. She straightens her shoulders and places her hand atop Marianne's head. "A gift for our junior members."

Marianne marvels at the three in similar fashion. "For me? But this is Charlotte's big day. I don't need a gift."

Aunt Winnie pinches Marianne's cheek. "If not for all the hours you put in, my Charlotte's dream would have taken a lot longer to come true. You're the one who pushed for this to happen. This is just as much your victory as it is Charlotte's."

I squeeze Marianne's hand, agreeing wholeheartedly. "You come over practically every other day after working at the library to help me bake. You're the one who helped me turn this into a business. They're right; you deserve whatever is in that envelope."

Marianne's caution turns to glee. "Shall we?"

Karen takes a sip of her juice. "If you don't open those things, I will."

I love these three wrinkled ladies who refuse to grow old. They're always up to something wild. "You didn't have to get me anything." The protest is weak, because I tear open the envelope with gusto, excited to get a gift. My mouth falls open when I pull out a certificate for...

I can't be reading this right.

"What is this? Aunt Winnie, did you seriously get us flying lessons?"

Marianne guffaws. "This is nice, but you know I'm afraid of heights."

Karen toasts us with her orange juice. "We sure do. Charlotte faced her fear of going into business for herself. You're next. There was a long waiting list, so those lessons won't actually happen until the spring. Plenty of time to gear yourself up for it."

Marianne looks like she might vomit. "You already booked it?"

Agnes grins, gleeful in her mischief. "We sure did. There's no backing out now."

Karen taps the edge of my gift certificate with her thin, knobby finger. "You've proved that you're Charlotte the Brave by opening the Bravery Bakery. And you've shown that you're Marianne the Wild by pushing through any resistance to make this happen. Since the sky is the limit with qualities like that, we figured you should start working on crashing any limits that the sky might have in store for you."

The poetic sentiment rings through my body, jerking my heart to the forefront.

Agnes kisses Marianne on the cheek, and then me. "Big life moments deserve to be commemorated." She holds onto Marianne's hand. "You can do it, Marianne. Then when the two of you fall in love with flying and get your pilot licenses, you can fly us all over the place. We'll be world travelers."

I snicker at their grand plans and even grander imaginations. "So this is actually a gift for you, right?"

Agnes winks at me. "All the best ones are."

Though I've never set my sights on learning to fly, the prospect of someday learning sounds like a lot of fun—scary though it may be. "Thank you so much. I can't wait to give this a try." And I truly mean it.

"This is your moment, girls." Aunt Winnie postures, looking on us with pride. "Use it unwisely."

Marianne holds my hand under the table, no doubt just as

spooked as I am that this is what constitutes an appropriate gift these days. I can tell that when the lessons near, Marianne is going to do her best to find a way out of this.

Which means it will be my job to make sure she gives it a try.

Aunt Winifred squeezes my shoulder. "Hurry up and finish eating, honey cake. That waitressing job isn't going to up and quit itself."

Karen leans her elbow on the counter. "I can't believe you're giving your two weeks instead of just quitting. At this rate, that halo of yours is never going to be tarnished." She tsks me, shaking her head as if I have completely missed the point of life.

I chuckle in her direction. "I have to go there anyway. I left my sweater there yesterday. Besides, I don't want to leave Bill in a lurch."

Winifred snickers into her morning tea. "My little rule follower. Whatever shall we do with you?"

It's an effort, but I manage to get myself out the door without being late for my shift. I have pink lipstick kiss marks on my left cheek from all the times Agnes smooched me, and red on my right cheek from the many times Aunt Winnie pinched me with her semi-arthritic grip.

The high of being sent off on this momentous day crests on the drive into work, and crashes completely when I get into the diner before it has opened to the public for the day. I hate letting people down, and I'm no good at confrontation.

I glance around the diner, noticing Judy's old brown clunker, Heather the hostess' silver coupe, the cook's mini-van and Bill's truck in the parking lot, along with my red sedan. Judy missed her shift yesterday, which put Bill in a bad mood. I'm glad she's here today, so Bill doesn't go off on a rant about responsibility before I can get a word in.

My steps are slow yet determined as I march into the diner

in the early dawn light, my black apron tied around my waist and a no-nonsense look on my face.

"Morning, Heather," I greet the teenaged hostess, who pops her pink gum without looking up at me. Heather occupies herself by scribbling on a notepad with her headphones on, tuning out the rest of the world as she always does before the shift starts.

I don't see Judy, who usually spends her minutes before we open sitting in a booth in the corner, writing in a journal with unmitigated focus. I hope she's not chatting with Bill. I really need to talk to him before I lose my nerve.

I summon up my courage and march into the kitchen, my voice louder than it should be. "Bill? Bill, I need to talk to you."

Bill is busy beside the line cook. He barely glances up when I speak. "If it's about asking for a raise, you can skip it. Heather and Judy both made their opinions clear in the past two weeks. If you get on my back about the pay, too, I might lose it."

I should probably learn how to interact with Bill without rolling my eyes, but the man has an uncanny knack of bringing out the teenager in me. "Could we talk in private? Like, sitting down?"

Bill squints at me. "We can talk exactly as we are. What's so important you have to slow down the morning prep, Charlotte?"

I envisioned quietly sitting in his office, explaining how grateful I am that he took a chance on me—a girl with no wait-ressing experience. He gave me a job when I was new in town and needed someone to hire me. I have a speech prepared about ambition, complimenting him on his own and how it led him to run Bill's Diner. Then I planned to segue into telling him I am going to open my own cupcake bakery.

In my imagination, he is proud of me.

But that beautiful moment I dreamed naïvely of crumbles before my eyes when I blurt out an uncouth, "Bill, I'm putting in my two week's notice." My voice quiets as his knife stills. "If that's okay."

Bill narrows his eyes at me. "Two weeks?"

"Yes, sir. Thank you for..."

But I don't get out my gratitude before Bill waves off my words. "Fine, fine. Can you refill the ketchup bottles? Judy was supposed to do it yesterday, but she was a no-show. If she pulls that again this morning, I'll be out two waitresses."

Well, I guess there's no love lost between us. "Sure thing. I saw her car in the lot. I'll go get her, then I'll see to the ketchup. Thanks for everything, Bill."

And I truly mean it. I am grateful for this smelly, outdated place.

I am also grateful to be moving on.

I trot out to the dining area, glancing around to Judy's usual morning booth. "Heather, has Judy come in yet?"

Heather shrugs, her eyes still on her notepad. "I don't see her, so I guess not."

As employees, we are not an enthusiastic bunch. Poor Bill.

I can't believe I just quit. I actually did it. I worried last night when I had trouble falling asleep that I might chicken out. But I did it.

I was Charlotte the Brave.

And now I've got to tell Judy that she might have to handle more tables if Bill can't replace me in the next two weeks.

I check the women's bathroom and then decide to go back out into the parking lot. I like how the air feels in the morning before the sun has had its chance to do its best. The early October air has shifted to bring a slight nippiness, making me think my purple knitted sweater I left here yesterday might not be enough to get me through the autumn season once it sets in more fully. I like how nature wakes me up, even if it leaves a chill on my skin.

My steps are quick as I jog out toward Judy's brown clunker, noting that the bumper is still askew. I didn't realize how useful duct tape could be; it's held her bumper on for at least as long as I've worked here.

I knock on Judy's window, donning a chipper smile. The glass is slightly fogged, but I see her outline in the driver's seat. She doesn't make to open the door, so I wait a few seconds, expecting some sort of response.

Maybe she's finishing up a phone call?

But there's no sound coming from inside the car.

After two more knocks, I worry she has fallen asleep. Poor thing. I wonder if she was a no-show yesterday because she was sick, and now she's come back to work too soon. She should go home and get some proper sleep.

I open her car door to tell her as much. "Judy? Hun, you should wake up. You'll catch a chill, napping in your car like this."

The sun isn't much help this early in the morning, but the light from the inside of her car shines down, illuminating parts of her that still my words and steal my breath.

Pink, bubbly vomit has slicked and dried all down her front. Her lips are painted red, but there is a discoloration around her mouth that infuses true fear in my soul.

"Judy?" My pulse quickens as I call her name in a whisper. "Judy! Judy, wake up!"

Her head lolls to the side, and for the first time, I realize her eyes are lidded but not closed.

Please let her be sleeping with her eyes open.

My fingers move slowly to her neck, feeling for a pulse, but nothing stirs beneath my fingertips.

My heart pounds so loud that I don't hear myself shouting her name over and over, even as I stumble back from her lifeless body. I grab my phone, dropping it twice before I take a picture of the scene and then call the police, hoping they will tell me that what I am seeing isn't what is real.

Please don't let it be real.

Judy made it to the parking lot, but she will never work another shift at Bill's Diner ever again.

2

LOST AND FOUND

*a*n officer presses a cup of coffee into my hand, though I'm not sure it's caffeine that I need. Seeing a dead body before the sun has started its workday has me wide awake. It feels strange to be sitting in one of the booths at Bill's Diner. I am hardwired to be bustling about, waiting tables and helping out. But given that Sheriff Flowers is sitting across from me, pen and notebook in hand, I don't think the diner will be opening any time soon.

"What made you go out to her car?" the sheriff asks, as if I need a reason for such a thing.

I quirk my brow at him, but Bill answers for me, putting a voice to my indignation. He folds his arms across his chest. "I did. Charlotte discovered the body because I asked her to go get Judy. We thought she was dozing in her car. Any other brilliant, borderline accusatory questions?" He stands between us, staring down the sheriff.

I have never been more grateful for Bill's surly demeanor in all my life.

The sheriff jots something down and directs the next question at the two of us, instead of just me. "Did Judy often fall asleep in her car before work?"

"No, but she didn't show up to work yesterday." I hold tight to my mug. "I assumed she'd had the flu and perhaps came back to work too soon." I glance around. "That's not too crazy, right?" I gnaw on my lower lip.

Bill glares at the sheriff. "Not crazy at all. You're wasting your time in here, Sheriff. The dead body is out there in the parking lot."

The sheriff tilts his head up at Bill. I can practically see him cementing his backside more firmly in the bench opposite mine, as if the challenge to his authority triggers a stubbornness in him that refuses to be quelled. "I've got people covering that. I'm in here, asking the questions. What do you think about Judy, Bill? Was she often a no-call no-show? I'll bet that got irritating."

Bill rolls his eyes. "Is this how you actually do policework? Are you hoping I'll confess to a murder with that grand opening? Honestly. I've got customers waiting for their breakfast, and employees who serve their best coffee when they're not being harassed." He motions out the big picture window to the people crowded on the other side of the crime scene tape.

My stomach roils for many reasons, not the least of which is a navy pickup that crawls into the lot, allowed in by one of the officers. My heart leaps into my chest. Though Logan and I have been on a handful of dates and we talk or text nearly every day, I still haven't managed to shake the butterflies that swarm whenever he comes into view. The sheriff's son isn't an unexpected presence, given that Logan is an officer, but his face still manages to captivate me when he gets out of his truck.

He doesn't move towards the crime scene, but jogs into the diner, his green eyes widened and a winded look to him. "I came as soon as I heard," he explains when his eyes lock in on mine. For as new as we are to each other, I don't mind one bit when he tugs me out of the booth and wraps me in a giant hug. Warmth sinks into my skin, patching over the spots of me that went cold at the sight of Judy.

"She was in her car. I thought she was sleeping! I opened the door and gave her shoulder a little shake, and she fell forward, and that's when I realized she was dead." I burrow my face into his shoulder. "It was awful."

Logan's hand spans the breadth of my back. "I called Marianne on my way in. She'll be here soon, but until she gets here, I'm not leaving your side."

Have sweeter words ever been spoken? If they have, I'm not sure I've heard them.

The sheriff stands, clearing his throat. "I think I'll make myself useful outside."

Bill grumbles something that sounds like, "That's more like it." Then he turns to me, no less surly than he was when he was directing his displeasure at the sheriff. "You put in your two-week notice. I want every minute of those two weeks of work, young lady. So get yourself together. As soon as that police tape lifts, we're opening those doors."

He says it like a threat, causing me to bristle as he walks away toward the kitchen. "I know, I know."

Logan opens his mouth to say something, but his words never hit the air. Marianne's voice fills the diner, lifting my spirits when she calls my name. "Charlotte! Oh my goodness. Charlotte! Are you okay?"

The hugging starts all over again, only I can't exactly lean my head on Marianne's dainty shoulder, as she is several inches shorter than I am. Still, the solace is real and quite necessary. Her olive skin hasn't lost a bit of the sun we bathed in two days ago, even though I've already paled. Her hair is worn in two long brown braids that swoosh over her shoulder when she releases me to get a handle on the situation. "Tell me everything," she insists.

Even though I've just gone over it all twice now, I delve into the muck a third time for my best friend's sake. By the time I finish, she's got me gathered up in another hug. "This was supposed to be your freedom day, not a crime scene! Did you do it?" She leans in, glancing around to make sure Bill isn't nearby. "Did you put in your two weeks?"

I nod, chewing on my lower lip. "Yes, but I can't quit now. Bill is down a waitress." I shake my head. "Oh, poor Judy. I can't even begin to guess who could have done such a thing. She was a..." But I can't say she was a sweet woman because honestly, I have no idea. Our interactions were relegated to work talk and nothing more. We didn't even sit around complaining about Bill, though there was plenty of fodder for that. She stuck to her side of the diner and I worked on my side. "I was so happy to be done with my shifts that I left the second I could. I didn't actually know her barely at all." Regret washes over me.

Marianne squeezes my hand. "Well, let's get to know her, then. That's not impossible." Marianne casts around the diner. "She worked this section. She always wore black shorts or black pants and a t-shirt."

Yep, my list ends right about there, too.

Marianne casts around, looping her arm through mine while Logan trails on my other side. She walks me through Judy's section.

I motion to a booth in the corner. "That's where she sat in the morning, rolling silverware when she was waiting for the diner to open. Always had a notebook with her that she wrote in."

Marianne's mouth pulls to the side. "I want that notebook. Logan?"

Logan tips his head to Marianne. "On it. You got Charlotte?"

Marianne salutes Logan. "Yes, Officer."

I need Marianne for pretty much every step I take right now, since this day did not end up turning out as planned. She leads me to Judy's morning pre-shift booth. It feels odd and border-line discourteous to sit down in Judy's preferred seat, but we do it anyway. It feels respectful somehow to retrace her steps, knitting us that much closer to the deceased.

"She sat here, back to the rest of us, writing in her notebook. Sometimes she would stare out the window, but nothing more than that." I press my forehead to the tabletop. "I knew nothing about her."

Marianne frowns. "How did you find her? Like, in what state?"

I lift my head, quirking my brow. "Dead?"

"Not that." Marianne waves her hand between us to start over. "I mean, what sort of dead? Did she have bruising around her neck? Any telling marks?"

I grimace, not wanting to conjure it all back up. Instead of answering, I tug out my phone and hand it to her. "Here. The picture might be helpful."

Marianne purses her lips. "Oh, my. Poor thing." She zooms in on the center of the photo. "Is that her lipstick smeared? I can't tell."

I grind my knuckles into my temples. "Discoloration. It's like a purplish bluish around her lips. Not sure what could cause that. Vomit all down her front, but she'd fallen forward before I took the picture, so I'm not sure you can see it."

Marianne closes her eyes in a show of true sadness. "Oh, that's awful. Do you think she was poisoned?"

I nod, not wanting to go there in my mind. "I can't imagine what else the cause of death could be."

Marianne squeezes my hand. "Let's get you home. There's no

way the diner is opening any time soon. Murder on the premise means everyone gets a day off."

I wish Bill saw it that way. "Bill is certain we'll reopen soon."

Marianne stands, determination plain on her face. "Bill is incorrect. Get your things and let's go."

I stand and do as Marianne says because honestly, I don't have any bravery left in my bucket. After quitting and then stumbling upon a murder? There is no way I will make it through a shift of serving stale coffee.

I grab up my purse but turn toward the hostess stand. "Hold up. I need to check the Lost and Found for my sweater. I left it here yesterday." Heather must have already gone home. I don't know how she can slip out of here without fearing Bill's frustration, but I admire her take charge attitude. I should have left the second the sheriff went back to the parking lot.

I tug out the narrow bin that lives in bottom cubby of the hostess stand, shoved underneath extra menus and spare napkins. My lavender sweater was knitted for me by Agnes. It has pearl buttons and makes my skin look like it's glowing.

Once I get the menus and napkins out of the way, a sigh of relief leaves my lungs. "Oh, good." It stinks of French fry oil, but that's nothing a good washing can't fix.

My gaze catches on another item in the bin. My breath stills when I spot Judy's green notebook.

"Is that..." Marianne asks, lowering her voice to a tensed whisper.

I nod. "I think so. Judy wrote in it nearly every day."

Marianne's fingers trail over the word "Journal" written on the front. "I want to know what's in there."

It's a violation of Judy's privacy to take it out of the Lost and Found box. It's an even bigger issue that I slide it into my purse when I know the police might want to dig through her diary, or whatever it is that's written in here. But my curious side takes over. Before I know it, I'm waving goodbye to a disgruntled Bill and walking with Marianne out the front door.

I want to know this woman. I need to know what made her smile, because I never saw that particular facial expression at work. I want to know what made her come alive.

And I really want to know if there is anything in here that might point me in the direction of her killer.

3

STOLEN DIARY

*T*he nape of my neck is damp when we make it to the white colonial with beautiful pale blue shutters where I live with my Aunt Winifred. "We should turn this in, so the police can leaf through it," I tell Marianne for the third time this morning.

She shuts the front door behind us and calls through the home. "Winifred?" When no one answers, she lowers her shoulders. "We will, if there's anything worth reporting. Would you want a bunch of cops reading your diary?"

"No, but I also wouldn't want my coworkers reading it, either."

"This is purely investigative," Marianne argues, forcing conviction into her tone.

Winifred comes in from the backyard, her hands dirty from gardening. "Hello, girls. Well, don't you look taller. Must be all that chasing your dreams." She pinches my cheek. I'm guessing she leaves a dirt smudge on my face, but I don't bother wiping it off.

"We stole something," I confess, unable to exist in the same room as my aunt with a guilty conscience.

Marianne sighs, no doubt exasperated that I didn't make it one whole minute in the house without blurting out our crime.

Aunt Winnie's movements slow. I don't expect her to chuckle, but that's the sound that comes out of her mouth. "Is that so? Was it fun?"

I gape at her. "I should be in trouble! It wasn't fun. It's a crime!"

Aunt Winnie reaches for her phone, speaking into it before she addresses my impending panic attack. "Karen, come on over. Yeah, bring Agnes, too. Our girls have already committed their first felony. They might need a pro around because they're turning chicken real fast." She ends the call and then washes her hands in the kitchen sink. "Alright, honey cakes. What is it you two have stolen? Do you need an alibi?"

Marianne covers her face and groans. "I don't know what we were thinking, coming here. Charlotte is right; we stole something. It doesn't belong to us." She lowers her hands and hugs herself around the middle. Her teeth worry her lower lip. "Then again, Judy is dead, so the journal technically doesn't belong to anyone." She peeks at me, culpability shining through. "Would it be so wrong to open it?"

A groan sneaks out of me. "You're supposed to be the morally strong one! If you fold, then what do I have to hold onto?"

Aunt Winnie squeezes my shoulder. "I'll be your moral compass."

My chin angles downward, a wry look crossing my face. "Then we're doomed for sure."

Marianne inches toward the journal, taking a seat at the kitchen table. "Well, if we're already doomed, then one peek won't hurt."

"Solid logic." My dubious gaze lands on the journal, knowing I shouldn't invade Judy's privacy.

Aunt Winnie has no such qualms. The second Agnes and Karen step through the door, she flips open the journal.

I sigh, locking eyes with my goldfish, who is probably the only morally strong one left in the room, as I am about to give in. "Buttercream," I say to my fish, "this is your last chance to stop this from happening."

My fish flicks its tail at me in response, which isn't supremely helpful.

Karen takes the seat I offer her while Agnes gives both Marianne and me a hearty hug. That woman knows how to squeeze the sadness out of a person. She is pure love and doesn't hold back her big, beautiful heart. "I'm so sorry you had to find Judy like that. I knew her mother years ago. I should have checked on the girl more after her mother passed."

I know nothing about Judy, but now I crave the details. "She lived alone? When did her mother die?"

"Oh, years ago. A decade, maybe. Heart attack, poor dear. Judy kept the house, but it wasn't the same after her mother was gone."

I remain in Agnes' arms because part of me is still a little girl that craves a safe place. "What do you mean?"

Karen answers my inquiry as she takes the tea Aunt Winnie offers. "Oh, the shrubs are overgrown. The mail piles up on occasion. The grass doesn't get mowed. Things like that. Nothing terrible, but nothing her mother would have tolerated, either."

"Sounds like Judy was overwhelmed. It must be hard taking care of a house all by yourself. She didn't have a husband or any children?"

Karen shakes her head. "Never married. No kids. Keeps to herself mostly. Poor thing. Not exactly a friendly, chatty girl, but there's nothing wrong with that."

I can attest to that.

Marianne elbows me. "Show them the photo of the body." Then to the Live Forever Club, she says, "There was discoloration around her mouth and her front was covered in vomit."

Agnes closes her eyes, clutching me tighter. "Poisoned. Who would do such a thing? Judy never caused trouble."

Karen smacks her palms together and rubs them like she is washing with invisible soap. "Alright, ladies. Let's see what Judy has to tell us about herself."

I close my eyes, remaining in Agnes' arms. Normally I would be busying about the kitchen right about now, but apparently I have reverted back into a five-year-old, where I trust the adults have all the answers, and I won't leave their side until I am certain the waters are safe.

Karen perches her reading glasses on the edge of her nose and begins reading aloud to us.

"Dear Diary,

I'm not sure I can keep going like this. Things need to change, but I don't know how to make that happen. Money is so tight; I took leftovers home from the diner so I would have something to eat. Bill is a terrible cook, but it's better than going hungry again."

Whatever giggly mischief existed in the kitchen prior to those words hitting the air dissipates now.

Aunt Winnie clutches the fabric over her heart. "Oh, my. Poor dear. I had no idea."

Agnes grips me tighter with one arm and reaches to Marianne to bring her in with her other. "Girls, do you have enough to eat? Are you having any sort of trouble making ends meet?"

If I was in a more lighthearted mood, I would scoff. As it is, I simply answer honestly. "Aunt Winnie won't let me pay her any rent, so I've got nothing to complain about."

Aunt Winifred raises her chin defiantly. "Non-negotiable. You help me around the house and in the yard. That's payment enough."

We had this argument when I first moved in. To push it further now is fruitless.

"I barely have any bills, and the cupcake business is booming," I tell Agnes.

Marianne grimaces. "I have more than enough. I have so much that I could have helped Judy, had I known."

I glance around the room, knowing that poverty is not restricted to any particular age bracket. "What about you girls? Would you tell us if you ran into trouble?"

Karen chuckles. "I'm usually running headfirst into trouble. But no, we're all fine. That's the beauty of being beautifully aged."

I can't believe I've never asked if I can be more helpful to them. They basically saved me, reinvented me, and showed me I can be more than I ever dreamed.

Karen continues reading, introducing us to Judy's dire situation that, over many months of her writing, only seemed to get worse.

Karen pauses, frowning at the page.

"I DON'T KNOW ABOUT GOING TO A BOOKIE. THE WHOLE THING SEEMS scary. But Frank promised me that betting on the football game is easy. I don't have much to lose. Please let this work."

. . .

MY MOUTH DROPS OPEN AS A PRICKLE OF POSSIBILITY CREEPS OVER my skin. "Judy started betting on sports games? Did I miss the part where she was all about football before this?"

Aunt Winnie shakes her head, halfway through her second cup of tea. "I think we need to talk to Frank."

Marianne and I lock gazes, certain there is more to Judy's death than anyone could possibly have guessed.

4

BETTING AGAINST A KILLER

Frank and I have been on a first name basis for a while now, mostly because of his flower box. Most of the businesses in Sweetwater Falls have the same oblong flower boxes hanging outside of their windows. Frank's stand doesn't have windows, but on the side of his checkout area, he's got purple flowers with white daisies that always look happy and welcoming.

These are my favorite flowers in all of Sweetwater Falls for the sole reason that Logan sneaks me secret notes between the petals.

But today, sniffing the flowers and plucking out my letter is not the first thing on my mind. I need to talk to Frank before I see if Logan has left me a letter in the flower box.

"Morning, Frank," I say in a sing-song voice. "How are you today?"

Frank nods at me, counting singles before he lays them flat in the register. "Not as sunshiny as usual, I'm afraid. Did you hear about Judy?"

I lower my head. "I did. I'm the one who found her, actually."

Frank's brows raise. "That's awful. I heard her neck was sliced open and her hands were bound."

I blanch at the graphic imagery. "Not at all. She had discoloration around her mouth and vomit down her front. Who told you that her throat was cut?"

Frank shakes his head. "Oh, you know how people talk."

I narrow my eyes at him. "Well, tell Delia to get her story straight before spreading heightened fear around like that." I can guess with some certainty that the woman known for spreading town gossip is most likely his source of information, being that Frank has a crush on her.

Frank chuckles as he takes a stack of magazines out and slits open the package with a box cutter. "Now how do you know it's Delia who's talking?"

I shoot him a wry look. "Seriously? You really want me to answer that?"

Frank smirks at me, a lock of dark, oily hair falling to his forehead. "Not really. I'll set Delia straight when she comes back around. You missed her this morning, though. Already came by." His blue jeans are worn and his shirt untucked, but the look is completely Frank, so I find it lightly endearing.

"Funny how Delia comes by your stand nearly every day." I thumb through the magazine I have no interest in buying. "Ever think of asking her out?"

That's a clear yes, but Frank guffaws. "No. She wouldn't... I'm not..." When he finishes spluttering, he glares at me good naturedly. "Are you planning on buying anything, or did you just stop by to see if Logan left you a love note?"

"Well, I didn't stop by just for that." I don't know how to deftly work what I want to say into the conversation, so I go with a total and utter lie. "Frank, I worked with Judy, and she mentioned you introduced her to a bookie. I was hoping to make some extra money to help with expenses for my cupcake business. Is there a way you could..." I am completely out of my element with this fib and have no clue how to make my request sound natural. "Could you get me in on the next game?"

I want to know how this works. How bad it all gets. If Judy couldn't pay her bookie, is he the sort to get violent?

Frank raises an eyebrow at me. "Do you know much about football?"

Enough to lose a few bets, sure. "I would imagine an educated guess seems about as fruitful as an uneducated one in these types of situations."

Frank chuckles at my logic. "I don't recommend it, but I can give you his number if you're really sure this is something you want to try."

"I'm really sure."

Frank takes out a scrap piece of paper from the small garbage and scribbles down a string of digits. Before he hands it to me, he holds it in the air between us. "I don't feel good about giving this to you. You've got that nice girl way about you."

"Nice girl way? What way is that, exactly? I'm not going around kicking puppies or anything, but I'm okay taking a risk here and there."

Another lie. Even having this conversation makes me anxious.

Frank smirks at me, as if I've said something comical. "Gambling can be fun, but it can also get dark if you don't know what you're doing. Judy didn't get out when I told her to, and she got in over her head."

This much, I know. When Karen read to us the portions of her diary toward the end, it was a progression of higher bets and bigger losses. Her last entry ended with, "After tomorrow, everything will be better."

It was either a suicide note, or a false hope that the bet she placed was going to pay off in a big way.

I hate thinking Judy killed herself. I need to know if she won her last big bet or if she lost, and consequently lost her life. If she won, I cannot imagine she would take her own life, or that the bookie would come after her.

I put the magazine back on the rack, admiring the selection of candy. "All the wrappers are Halloween themed. That's cute. So much fuss over a silly kids' holiday."

Frank scoffs at me. "Them's fighting words around here, new girl. Halloween is a big deal in Sweetwater Falls."

I glance around, noticing the fall decorations hanging on the light posts, but there's nothing particularly Halloween about the décor. "Really? I wouldn't have guessed."

Frank follows my gaze and waves his hand dismissively. "Tomorrow is October first. That's when the fall decorations switch to Halloween. There's a big festival toward the end of the month in the town square. The Spook Booths. The contest for the businesses who all try to make their building the scariest." He leans in to gage my reaction. "Any of this ringing a bell?"

"Sorry. I've been bogged down with Judy's death. Haven't thought much about Halloween. I didn't realize people got super into it here." The wheels in my mind start turning in a new direction. "Maybe I should come up with a Halloween-themed cupcake to sell."

"Maybe?" Frank scoffs. "Definitely. And I'd be prepared for them to sell out. I've heard nothing but good things about your cupcakes. Your clients are going to want something festive." He taps his noggin. "Know your audience."

I glance around for inspiration, knowing that I need to nail this flavor, whatever it might be. "Not pumpkin. That's overdone and the consistency is difficult to nail every single time." I do my best to halt my grudge against cooking with pumpkin. "Although there's nothing better than a pumpkin spice latte in the fall. Mm."

Frank snickers at my musing. "Good luck finding that around these parts. Can I be there when you try to order a pumpkin spice latte? I want to see the face of the waiter. I bet it'll look something like this." Frank contorts his features to look as if I've just requested pickled liver on a donut sandwich.

"It's not that weird. But no pumpkin cupcakes. I'll think of something better." I select a magazine on knitting for Agnes. "Has Agnes picked this one up yet?"

"Nope. It's new this week."

I pay the few dollars for the magazine, then wait for Frank to be distracted with a new customer before I meander to the flower box and sift through the petals.

No love note.

I try not to look too put out. Logan is working on Judy's case. I should be glad he's not wasting time writing to me.

I tug an envelope out of my pocket and fold it in half, leaving a note for Logan to find the next time he stops by.

My mind is whirling when I walk away from the Nosy Newsy. Cupcake flavors, a possible murderer, the question of suicide and the Halloween festival all swim around in my brain, each topic fighting to take up first place on my list of things to obsess about.

Though I want to solve Judy's murder as soon as possible, I know I won't be able to do that unless my hands are busy baking.

I make my way to the library, hoping to puzzle through my conundrums with Marianne by my side to help me make sense of it all.

5

CINNAMON AND PUMPKIN

*S*taring at the spices on the long shelf at the Colonel's General store should solve it all, but even after five minutes of concentration, all I have managed to do is zone out.

"How about cinnamon?" Marianne suggests.

My shoulders tighten. "Cinnamon is a crutch." My words come out harsher than I mean for them to. Instant shame washes over me. "I'm sorry. It's a good suggestion. I'm in a bad headspace, is all."

Marianne sets the cinnamon back on the shelf with the demeanor of a puppy who's been scolded. "You know more about baking than I ever will. What does your gut tell you?"

"I'm completely stuck." I pinch the bridge of my nose. "There are no bad ideas in brainstorming, yet your first suggestion I throw out the window. It's not you; it's me. I can't seem to think in a straight line. Cupcakes should be fun and flow easily. I could do a flavor I've done before. No one will care."

"People love pumpkin," Marianne suggests brightly. "And Halloween is all about pumpkins. Pumpkin pie, Jack-o-lanterns..."

She's right, but I don't want to do it. Pumpkin is the obvious choice, and one I don't want to make. Plus, baking with something so heavy and wet isn't my forte. I can't seem to get consistently good results. If the orders pour in for the new flavor of the month as they have for the other varieties, consistency is high on the list of things that matter.

But being that I just rudely shot down Marianne's suggestion of cinnamon, I don't want to condemn her second idea so quickly.

"Maybe," I offer noncommittally. "Talk to me about the Halloween Festival. Maybe that will spark some ideas."

She tells me the same things Frank does but adds a few details for my mind to latch onto. "Dwight dresses up in a pumpkin costume. It's so huge, he can't put his arms down. He spends the whole festival trying to shake hands with people and missing his mark. He accidentally slapped one of Dennis and Laura's kids one year. Not that he didn't deserve it. Those kids are terrible." She chuckles at the memory. "There's a booth where you can bob for apples. There's a contest for the kids where they string donuts up on a line stretched across two poles. The kids have to try to eat them without using their hands, and without the donut falling off the string. Winner gets a huge donut. Then they do a round for the adults, which gets highly competitive." She holds out her hands. "I mean, the prize donut you win is at least two feet in diameter. I never win, but it's my dream."

I didn't think there was anything that could make me love Marianne Magnolian more than I already do, but that tips it. "Your dream is to win the giant donut? That is totally cute."

Her eyes go round as she explains the difficulty involved in achieving something so grand. "Last year, my donut didn't fall off the string, but I wasn't fast enough. There's a balance you have to strike between taking care you don't knock the donut off, while also rushing to make sure no one else finishes before you."

I try to iron out a giggle, so she doesn't think I'm laughing at her cuteness. I adore her. "Well, then it sounds like we've got some work to do."

"Huh?"

"We've got less than a month, Marianne. If you want to get your speed and dexterity up to snuff, we need to practice."

Marianne laughs. "I don't think eating donuts is a thing people need to practice."

"It's your dream!" I protest. "You are getting that giant donut prize this year. I'll make sure of it." I cast around the aisle but then grimace. "You don't want store made donuts. I'll make you some, and every time you come over to bake, we can practice."

"You know how to make donuts?"

I blow a raspberry at her question, though, to be honest, it's been a hot minute since I've made donuts. "Please. I'm not a one-trick pony. Cupcakes are my passion, but I can do a mean cake, donuts, cookies, you name it. For you? I'll become the best donut maker there ever was."

Marianne waves off my offer. "You don't have to make them from scratch! I made too big a deal out of it. It's silly."

Seriousness floods me, pushing out any hint of a tease. I reach over and grip her wrist. "It's not silly; it's your dream. We are going to get you ready for the competition. They won't know what hit them."

Marianne lets out a giddy squeal of delight. "Really? You'll help me train for this?"

"It will be the most fun anyone has ever had training for anything. There are donuts involved. I'm in."

Marianne bobs on the balls of her feet and claps her hands a few times. "I can't wait!"

I turn back to the spice section, my smile twisting into an expression of sheer contemplation. "The Halloween Festival sounds fun. I love how many little events they pour into each gathering. So much work and planning goes into these festivals. Very cool."

"There's a Spook Booth contest, too. The Live Forever Club always has the scariest one."

"What's a Spook Booth?" Frank mentioned it earlier, but I still have no idea what it is.

"I don't want to tell you about it; you'll just have to see for yourself." She shudders, piquing my interest.

"Can't wait."

Marianne keeps her eyes on the spices, picking one up at random. "I was thinking of inviting Carlos to the Halloween Festival."

I smirk at her cuteness. "I think that's a great idea. You haven't seen him since our double date last month. Is he still a smitten kitten?"

Marianne's neck shrinks. "Maybe." She motions to the wall of tiny jars, reaching for an abrupt change of topic. "None of these spices are singing to you?"

I sigh. "Pumpkin cupcakes are hard for me to keep fluffy and light. I can do a yellow cake with pumpkin spice. That's usually cloves, nutmeg, cinnamon and ginger. Sometimes allspice. But all of that's been done."

"Not here, it's not." She keeps her eyes on the jar in her hand. "You were talking to Fisher about a pumpkin spice latte. Are those good?"

I turn slowly to her, my mouth falling open. "Are you serious? Pumpkin spice lattes are the one thing autumn was missing before they were invented. Every now and then, I debate driving out of town until I find one." I inhale, and it's like I can smell the comforting beverage and feel it warming my hands. "It smells better than a pumpkin pie and tastes like a hug."

Marianne leans her shoulder to the shelf, staring at me as if I've started reciting chapters from one of her favorite epistles. "I love when you get all poetic about food. That's the one you have to make. If you don't want to use pumpkin, then don't. Use the spices and flavor a yellow cake, or however that works."

"Pumpkin spice without the pumpkin is cheating," I counter, but my heart isn't in the debate. "But maybe I can do a pumpkin frosting to incorporate the pure pumpkin flavor. It might not be as pretty as a normal buttercream, but it's worth a shot." My nose crinkles. "Not buttercream. A cream cheese frosting would be best."

Marianne grins. "Now you're talking. You've got that look about you. That wistful gleam that says you're on the right track." She straightens the spice jars on the shelf. "Now we can start to figure out who killed Judy."

I blink at her abrupt switch in topic. "What?"

"You know you have a hard time concentrating on clues unless you're baking cupcakes. Let's buy what you need and get started. I've got theories." Her eyebrows dance, but when I ask her to tell me what her theories are, she holds up her finger. "Not until we're baking."

It's the fastest I've ever made it through a grocery store. There is nothing I want more than to get to the bottom of this and find Judy's killer.

6

BEDTIME STORIES FOR BUTTERCREAM

*F*iguring out a new recipe using an ingredient I am not overly fond of is an exercise in patience. It's akin to fighting with a lover or a friend, knowing in the end you have to land somewhere solid, but neither of you are willing to come to a compromise.

I stare at the can of pumpkin on the counter, scowling at it every so often as I get the other ingredients together.

Marianne takes out the groceries and puts them in the cheery, yellow-painted kitchen, making sure to leave out the eggs, cream cheese, butter and spices for me. "Do we have enough flour?" she asks me. "We're filling all the Friday cupcake orders tomorrow. Did you take a count to see how many dozen we're making?"

"I love that you say 'we'. Have I mentioned how grateful I am that you are my lovely baking assistant? I honestly don't know how I would get this all done without you."

"You've mentioned it only about a hundred times this week." Marianne grins when the backdoor opens. "Hey, Winifred. We're taking over the kitchen a day early so we can experiment with a new cupcake flavor."

Winifred casts us a tired smile. "Please let it be something I get to taste test. I deserve something sweet after the day I've had."

I pause my measuring and pull out a chair for my great-aunt. "What's going on?"

"Oh, I've been helping get things ready for Halloween. Lots of setting up stuff and hauling decorations from Ben's barn to the main stretch in town."

"I didn't know Sweetwater Falls decorated the streets. That's cute. More pumpkins and haybales?" I guess, turning on the kettle atop the stove, so I can make my sweet aunt some tea to warm her.

Aunt Winnie chuckles. "Haybales, sure, but the zombies that pop out of them are hard to get positioned just right. The pumpkins are huge. I don't help with those."

Marianne fills in the gaps of Aunt Winnie's explanation. "Every business sets out a pumpkin statue that they decorate themselves. It started out as real pumpkins, but you know how people get. The pumpkins got bigger and bigger, so most of the business owners switched to huge lawn ornaments of pumpkins. Last year, the Colonel put fireworks in hers that shot out at dusk every Friday night through October."

My eyes widen. "Yikes. So Sweetwater Falls really gets into Halloween, I take it."

Aunt Winnie rubs the back of her neck. "Oh, yes. It's a month-long celebration."

A knock on the front door turns my head toward the living room. "Are you expecting anyone?"

Marianne grins at me. "That'll be Logan. I texted him earlier to let him know we were experimenting with flavors. He volunteered to be the dishwasher for us again."

A bashful smile teases my lips. "He does that twice a week already. He doesn't have to do that tonight."

Marianne bats her hand in my direction. "He wants to see you, and you're still too chicken to ask him over. Plus, we need a wider opinion on this new flavor than just me and Aunt Winnie. We're not all that discriminating when it comes to sugar."

Aunt Winnie raises her hand. "Hear, hear."

Though Marianne invited Logan over, I decide to be brave and answer the front door. A smile sweeps over the two of us in unison when we greet each other. "It's good to see you, Logan. I know you have things to do. Thanks for coming by."

Logan doesn't come in but stands on the porch and motions for me to join him outside in the moonlight. "Walk with me?"

I pause, but since the oven isn't on and nothing is time-sensitive with the cupcakes, I acquiesce and step out onto the porch. It's slightly chilly, but I don't mind the breeze. "What's on your mind?"

"Oh, first, could you put this in the house?" He hands me a fishing magazine.

"What's this for?" I look it over, my lips pursed. "I didn't know you fished."

"Only when my dad makes me. It's to read to Buttercream later." When I tilt my head at him curiously, he explains. "I heard that reading to babies even before they know words is a good thing to do. It's got to be the same if you read to a fish, right? Maybe Buttercream will like the pictures. I don't want your goldfish to get spooked when I'm around because she doesn't recognize me. Got to put in the time."

I try to hide my smirk, but I can't suppress my delight in Logan's cuteness. "I think that's a nice idea." I flip open the magazine, grimacing at the image of the dead fish on a fisherman's line. "Maybe not this picture, though. Or this one," I add, turning to the next page.

Logan winces. "Oh, I didn't think of the snuff aspect of it all. I was just thinking of the open waters and swimming fish." He reaches for the magazine, his ears pinking at my teasing smile. "It was a bad idea."

I hold the magazine out of reach and set it on the end table in the living room. "No, no. It's sweet. Just make sure you look at the picture first before you show it to Buttercream. There are plenty of good ones in there to choose from." I step out onto the porch once more. "That's totally precious, Logan."

"I'll take 'totally precious' over 'idiot who reads a magazine about dead fish to a live fish.'"

"Precious," I insist.

Logan proffers his elbow to me, waiting for me to loop my arm through his before we set out on a stroll down the sidewalk. "I've been thinking about how much I enjoy spending time with you. We've had a few dates, and I've loved each one of them."

"Me too. Despite how clumsy I get around you, I look forward to seeing you now."

The corner of Logan's mouth lifts. "I like hearing that."

We pass by a tree whose leaves have turned all sorts of vibrant colors. Even in the dwindling evening's light, I can appreciate the varying hues.

Logan likes me in his space, I've learned. He keeps me close while we walk, and I couldn't be happier with the arrangement. His voice is low and quiet, strumming the strings of my heart with ease. "I'm not seeing anyone else. I don't want to, either. I'd like to only date you, if that's alright."

Though I assumed as much, it's nice to have confirmation. "Same. The more time I spend with you, the more I want to spend with you. Dating you is addictive, I suppose."

Logan makes this "mm" sound in his chest when he's content. I love that sound, and feel grateful I get to experience it now. "Glad to hear it. I was hoping you might go out with me Friday night. Just you and me."

We've had Marianne as our buffer on nearly every date we've

been on. At first, the buffer was completely necessary. I was (and still sometimes am) a colossal klutz around Logan. But he's right; it's been a few weeks of cute notes, flirty glances and double dates. Perhaps it's time we take the training wheels off this thing. "I wouldn't mind that. Thanks for waiting until you were sure I wouldn't trip over my own two feet."

Logan visibly relaxes, now that I've agreed. He turns us so we are walking back in the direction of the house. That I can make this man nervous about anything is a wonder I will never understand. "Now if I can just keep myself from making a fool of myself."

I shoot him a dubious look. "When do you imagine that happened? You've never done anything imperfect."

Logan laughs dryly. "One of the times I came to pick you up, I had my shirt on backwards. Winifred clued me in so I could fix it before you came downstairs. And I'm sure you've noticed the times my voice cracked."

I pull back, utterly flummoxed. "I never noticed any of those things."

Logan chuckles, shaking his head at himself. "I guess I'm too hard on myself. You don't mind going out with just me?"

I lean my temple to his shoulder. "I can think of worse ways to kill a Friday night."

Logan leads the way back to the porch and opens the front door, ushering me inside.

"You might not want to be here for cupcake baking tonight, though," I warn him. "I'm testing a new flavor."

"That sounds like a night I definitely don't want to miss."

"You say that now. You're about to get to know a whole new side of me."

He raises his brow and slides his jacket off his shoulders. "Is that so?"

"I get a little agitated if they don't turn out right. Fair warning."

"You'll be in good company, then. We're nowhere near solving Judy's murder, which is the sort of thing that agitates me. We'll be two pieces of human sandpaper tonight."

I love that he admits this flaw to me. "That sounds frustrating," I offer. "Anything I can do to help?" I debate admitting to him that Marianne and I found Judy's diary and are making plans to track down a possible suspect. It might be something he should know about. But if it turns out to be a dead end, then I will have wasted his time for nothing.

Logan runs his hands from forehead to chin as we linger in the living room. For the first time, I see how worn he looks. "It's starting to look more and more like a suicide. That hurts me on like, a soul level. I don't want to think that anyone in our town would be devastated enough to do something like that. It feels like a failure on the entire population of Sweetwater Falls, that we could let one of our own slip off the map like that."

I was going to head into the kitchen with him, but this peek into the recesses of his personality pings at my heart. I lead him to the couch so we can sit together. "That's heavy, Logan. It sounds like you're carrying around more than just the downsides of the job."

Logan leans back, threading his fingers through mine while he vents. "I went to school with Judy. We weren't in the same grade; she was two years older than me. But that's no excuse. I could have reached out." He shakes his head, appearing completely downtrodden. "Looking into her life, there's nothing that points to her death being a murder, and lots of warning signs that her death might very well have been self-inflicted. She was only thirty-seven years old, Charlotte."

There is nothing to say that could ease his pain. And truthfully, sometimes pain doesn't need to be prettied up. Oftentimes it needs to hit the air without judgment or expectation that it has no place in the world and must be banished without examination.

I hold Logan's hand, letting him feel the low of this possibility. The only thing I can offer is to not make him go through these emotions alone. "You've got a lot on your plate. Knowing the victim makes it that much harder."

Logan nods. "I made a list of all the people I went to school with who still live in Sweetwater Falls. That's what I did when I should have been sleeping last night. I'm going through the list one by one, visiting or calling each person to see how they're doing. Crossed one person off my list today. I have plans to go see another tomorrow."

"That's a really nice idea, Logan. You have a good heart."

Logan meets my gaze, meeting my affection with a forlorn melancholy he doesn't bother concealing from me. "If that were true, maybe Judy wouldn't have taken matters into her own hands."

I close my eyes, knowing I cannot keep Judy's journal a secret any longer. "Logan, we can't be sure that Judy committed suicide." I drag in a deep breath before laying out a piece of the puzzle I haven't known how to handle. "Marianne and I found Judy's journal. Her private diary."

Logan blinks at me, sitting straighter. "What?"

"There's nothing in there that suggests she had plans to kill herself. But we did find something else."

Logan's mouth falls open. "Are you serious? How long have you had this journal?"

I fight the urge to shrink at what I can see now is a poor decision. I steel myself because I just know we are about to have our first argument. "Since I found her. The journal was in the Lost and Found at the diner, so we took it home. I wasn't going to read it, but then…" I can't throw Aunt Winnie under the bus, so I don't finish my sentence.

Logan closes his eyes. "Charlotte, I'm trying to guess at the logic that led you to keep this from me."

That makes two of us. "I guess I thought I would have been embarrassed if I died, and my private diary was floating around a police station for a bunch of people to read."

"So you read it yourself?"

I chew on my lower lip while regret washes over me. "It was a bad decision. I should have turned it in to the police. To you."

Logan doesn't release my hand. He doesn't raise his voice or take things farther than this. "I'm sorry you didn't think you could come to me with this." He takes my hand and presses it to his heart. "We'll get there."

I expect an unleashing—a rant or something. But Logan sits beside me with kindness in his eyes and my hand on his chest.

"I kept a clue from you," I tell him. "You lost sleep because you were certain Judy killed herself, which isn't a certainty at all."

I keep waiting for Logan to lose his temper, but he merely nods. "You had your reasons."

I frown at him. "They weren't good ones."

Logan chuckles but doesn't smile. "That's not for me to judge."

I pull my hand away from him. "You're being nice to me."

Logan tilts his head to the side. "Would you rather I was mean?"

I study his sweetness, wondering how he came to be so steady, so gentle.

It's not the perfect moment, and I am certainly not the perfect girl, but I can't help myself. I reach out and stroke his prickly cheek, marveling that gentleness this pure is sitting on my couch right now. Maybe I should wait for our first date that isn't with Marianne. Maybe I should hold off for a moment better than this.

But the only thing that makes sense to me is closing the gap between us so I can kiss this beautiful man who lets me be imperfect without shame.

7

MEASURING AND DISHWASHING

$\mathcal{M}$y eyes are wide and my voice high-pitched when Logan and I walk into the kitchen hand in hand. "Logan's here," I announce, stating the obvious.

Marianne has a terrible poker face, even with her back turned to us. "Hi, Logan!"

Aunt Winnie looks up from her teacup, her smile beaming. "Well, Logan. I had no idea you were here."

Logan narrows his eyes at the two, pausing to take in their elation. "How long were you spying on us?"

Aunt Winnie sips her tea. "Long enough to know that one day, you two just might outdo the scandal that couch has seen in its lifetime. I've put it through white the workout on my dates over the years."

I balk at her frankness while Marianne breaks into giggles. "Finally! You two are so cute. So sweet. And now you're actually together!"

Logan doesn't let go of my hand, even though I wish I could melt into the floor to escape this conversation. "Alright, you two. Don't scare Charlotte away, now." He motions to the sink. "I was promised a sink full of dishes. That's like, two things."

He pulls a chair out for me, which is good timing, because my legs are wobbly. The term "weak in the knees" is a perfect descriptor for the state in which Logan's kiss left me.

Marianne sets down the mixing bowl, resting the wooden spoon inside. "I started on the plain yellow cake batter. You get to do the magic that makes this taste like a pumpkin coffee."

"Pumpkin spice latte," I remind her, finally coming back to myself and finding my voice.

"Right." Marianne opens the spice cupboard. "Which ones do you need? I know it's cinnamon, and don't make that face when I say 'cinnamon'," she says, her back to me. "You said it was one of the ingredients in pumpkin spice."

Logan chuckles as he turns on the faucet to wash the two dishes we have accumulated. "What's wrong with cinnamon?"

I stare into the cupboard. "It's a crutch. I mean, sure, it tastes good, but it's used in so many things. It makes me feel unimaginative. I can do better." I stand, resolving myself to do exactly that. "I *will* do better. Okay. We need ground ginger, nutmeg, cloves and allspice, too."

Marianne gets down the spices, cautioning me before she hands them over. "Measure, young lady. When you just toss things into the bowl, I can't copy that. I need to be able to be helpful, which means I need a recipe."

I give my best glum expression and pull out the measuring spoons. "Oh, fine."

Logan keeps his eyes on the dishes while he speaks. "So tell me about Judy's diary. What have we learned so far?"

Marianne's neck shrinks. "That we should have brought it to the police?"

Logan chuckles. "Sure, but I didn't mean that. I meant what did you learn about Judy? Miss Charlotte seems convinced that Judy didn't kill herself. Did you find anything in the diary to substantiate that?"

Marianne takes the dry ingredients and adds them to the wet ones. "We found toward the end that she started gambling. Finances were tight and bills were starting to add up. Frank introduced her to his bookie, and she placed a few bets."

I fill in the blanks while I measure the ginger with a heavy hand. "She won a couple, but then lost a lot. Judy owed the bookie quite a bit."

Marianne quotes a particularly memorable section in the diary. "'Where am I going to get a thousand dollars?'"

Logan's shoulders lower. "Oh, jeez. I didn't realize. Yeah, that's definitely something to take into consideration. I'll talk to Frank and get the name of the bookie."

I grimace, reaching for my purse. "You don't have to. I sort of already did. Here's his name and number." When I hand it over, I feel the need to defend myself, though Logan isn't looking at me with anything other than the same mild exasperation that he cast us earlier for being kept out of the loop. "What? I just so happen to be passing by the flower box at Nosy Newsy yesterday, and the topic came up."

Logan shakes his head, donning a wry smile to erase any hint of agitation. "You beat me there by a day. If you check the flower box now, I'm sure you'll find the daisies are particularly chatty."

A blush sneaks over my cheeks. I love that we have a secret in plain sight—letters exchanged like true romantics. "I might have to stop by there in the afternoon."

Logan pockets the slip of paper from Frank. "I'll look into this tomorrow."

Aunt Winnie moves to the cupboard and slides out a bag of the turmeric tea I got her a while back. "You can do that, or you can wait until the game on Sunday."

I turn slowly to look at her.

Aunt Winnie pours some hot water into her teacup. "I've never bet on a sports game before. It was fun!"

I balk at her. "You didn't!"

"Like you weren't contemplating doing the same thing? I did, and so did Karen and Agnes. One of us is bound to lose. I want to see what happens when a person doesn't pay up."

Logan doesn't opt for sweetness this time. "You do realize that you could end up like Judy, if that's what happened to her, right? I want to figure out how Judy died just as much as everyone else, but I'm not willing to put you, Karen and Agnes in danger to get there."

Aunt Winifred rarely looks unsure of herself, but Logan's reframing tips her confidence. "I don't think Judy was murdered, kids." She points to the top of the fridge, where we've been storing Judy's journal. "I think Logan is right. I think she killed herself."

My stomach hollows. "Why do you think that?"

"Listen to how dismal she sounds in here." Winifred flips to a page at random. "'Nothing is going right in my life. I don't know why I bother trying.' There's not a speck of cheer anywhere in these pages. I don't think the bookie did it. So the girls and I placed bets to gather more evidence so you can put this case to bed."

Logan closes his eyes as if praying for patience. "So we've got two theories so far, and we're working on narrowing them down. I can get on board with that. What I never ever want to hear is that you're doing something potentially dangerous."

Aunt Winnie reclaims her seat. "If I'm right, then it's not. If I win, I'll use my windfall of cash to buy you something pretty. Perhaps a big banner that reads 'Winifred is Right'."

Logan shakes his head and sits in one of the empty chairs at the round kitchen table. "And if you're wrong, what then?"

Aunt Winnie's mouth pulls to the side. "Well, that's never happened before, so I have no frame of reference."

Marianne giggles at the quip, but then does her best to sober. "Not funny, Winnie. Logan's right. Your safety matters." Then Marianne turns to me. "Remember to check the orders for all the cupcakes we'll be making tomorrow. We need to be sure we have enough flour."

"Oh, right. Thanks." I take out my phone and log into my email. I get out a pen and paper so I can do my twice-a-week task of writing down how many cupcakes I will need to bake, and which flavors I will be making.

I expected the orders to dry up after the first week or two, but it's been more than that, and the orders only seem to grow. It's not the same people ordering every time, either, but a wide range, along with a several repeat orders.

My mouth falls open when I get to the next email and see the customer's name staring back at me. Volume deserts me, but luckily all three of them are so considerate that they turn when I croak out the name. "Judy." I glance up, panicked and worried that I have received an email from someone who died this week. "Judy ordered a dozen assorted cupcakes." My breath catches.

Marianne looks ashen. "When did she place the order?"

Bile churns in my stomach as I scan the details. "The day before I found her dead."

Marianne slowly meets my horrified gaze. "If I was planning to end it all, I wouldn't order myself cupcakes."

Aunt Winifred sips her tea while concern paints her features. "I guess I might be wrong after all. Judy didn't kill herself; she was murdered."

8

GOOD MORNING GOSSIP

Though I have no patience or energy for the countless questions that bombard me at every table I wait on at the diner the next day, I do my best to keep a calm disposition. "What can I get you this morning?" I ask in what I hope sounds like a pleasant tone.

"Morning? It's well after noon, young lady," an older man replies, chuckling at my slip.

Is it the afternoon? Time has no meaning anymore. I haven't had a break all day, except to use the restroom once, to which Bill asked me if that was absolutely necessary.

I had some choice words for him.

The line is out the door with everyone waiting for a table in my section.

If they wanted a table in my section because Bill is a horrible waiter, that would be one thing. He's taken over Judy's section, and despite his menu never changing, he has little talent for being able to take down multiple orders and turn them in at a decent pace.

But no one is clamoring to get a spot in my section because they don't want to endure Bill's slow, shoddy service. They all want to ask me about Judy's death, to which I have been faithfully responding with a succinct, "It's not appropriate breakfast talk." I wish they took note of the scolding in my tone, but no one seems to care that I clearly don't want to discuss the topic.

Heather drums her pen on the hostess stand. "You'll have to wait to get a seat in Charlotte's section. There's the line." She points at the length of people peering in my direction while they wait to get a table.

My frown cannot be concealed as I march over to the hostess stand. "Heather, you have to stop doing that. Seat them wherever there is an opening. I can't wait on this many people. It's stressing me out to have everyone staring at me, watching me work."

Heather pops her pink gum. "I mean, they're asking specifically to sit in your section. What else am I supposed to do?"

I speak slowly to her, holding back my frustration. "Tell them no?" I say it like it's a suggestion, knowing how bratty I sound. "It's first come, first serve. Look. Bill has an empty table." I grab up two menus and escort the people next in line to the opening in Bill's section without waiting for permission or approval.

Heather harrumphs, looking every bit like the teenager she is. "Oh. Well, I could have done that."

I grit my teeth to keep from spouting off an attitude-laced, "I know!"

This place is a madhouse.

One and a half weeks before I'm out of here, I tell myself as I bus my table and turn it over for the next person. I try to focus on the upside. It's a good day for tips, that's for sure. I'll be leaving with plenty of money in my pockets, even after pooling my tips with Bill and Heather for the day.

But after the millionth time of replying with a wan, "That's not appropriate lunch talk," the remnants of my positivity are coming to an end.

When I seat a person I recognize, I should be happy to see a friendly face, but the town gossip isn't who I was hoping to run into today. "Hey, Delia. Good to see you. What would you like me to get you to drink today?"

Delia has the look of a lion spotting an injured gazelle about her. Her frizzy chestnut hair is in a high, tight bun, her eyes wide and focused solely on me.

I am tired, frazzled and ripe for the attack. "Oh, Charlotte. You look positively exhausted. All these people, clamoring to get at you. Sit down for a second, hun."

Though I know I shouldn't, I do exactly that. My feet groan at me, reminding me that no matter how comfortable my tennis shoes are, they were not meant to support me for seven hours with no reprieve. "Thanks." Though even as I sit, I keep my waitressing wits about me. "What would you like to drink?"

Delia tilts her head to the side, her lower lip jutting out. "I can't believe you're working today. If I'd found a dead body, I wouldn't leave my house for a month. You're a trooper, Charlotte McKay."

"Thanks. Not much of a choice, though. I mean, Bill is down to one dayshift waitress. I don't mind coming in while he looks for someone to fill Judy's shoes."

Delia leans in, and internally, I groan. "I know Bill doesn't pay all that much, and the tips here can be spotty, I'll bet. I heard that Judy asked Frank if she could borrow a hundred dollars. I mean, a hundred dollars! She has a job. What could she possibly need a hundred dollars for? And Heather told me she asked to borrow fifty bucks from Sally."

I have no idea who this Sally person is, or why anyone would confide in Delia, unless they wanted their business spread around town.

Though, if Sally and Frank were out a bunch of money and they were sore about it, Sally or Frank might be the type of people to turn Judy's name to mud.

I should probably look into that, if only to tell them to stop running Judy's name through the muck. It's hardly appropriate at any time, much less now that Judy is dead.

I sigh. I mean, Judy needed more than that to pay off her bookie. I'm sure every little bit helped. "I'm a bit slammed today, Delia. How about I get you some coffee?" Decaf, for sure. I've never seen a peppier person.

Delia nods. "And a garden salad." She motions to her form with a smile. "I'm watching my figure. I've got a date this weekend."

"Oh yeah?" My eye catches on a booth that needs my attention. I stand, distracted when I reply. "Where is Frank taking you?"

Delia freezes. "Frank? Frank and I aren't dating. Why would you think it was him I'm going out with?"

I grimace, nodding toward a woman who motions to flag me down. "Oh, my mistake. Who's the lucky guy?"

"Why would you think it was Frank?"

I'm just turned around and tired enough to answer honestly. "I dunno, Delia. Probably because he lights up whenever you come around. He smiles at you in that way old movie stars smile at the back of the head of the woman they fancy."

I bite down on my tongue to keep from further embarrassing Frank, though I can see that ship has sailed.

Delia balks at me, then slides her hand over her mouth as shock hits her in waves. "Are you serious? I never noticed."

The woman who notices everyone and everything is clueless to the obvious. The irony could keep the best human behavior experts busy for hours.

I hustle away to fill the orders of the next few tables, taking my time coming back to Delia. "Here's your coffee." Decaf, because obviously caffeine would be a bad choice for Delia.

"Thanks. I've known Frank for years. I mean, *years*. If he likes me, why didn't he ever say anything?"

I shrug, knowing I've already stuck my nose in where it doesn't belong. "Would you have said yes?"

Delia frowns. "I don't know. I've never thought about him in that way before."

"People tend not to bring up the subjects that make us most vulnerable. You might be Frank's weak spot." I meet her eyes with a slight scolding shining through. "Maybe that hundred bucks was Judy's weak spot, and she'd prefer it not spread around town." I know I'm being direct, but Delia's just about my five millionth interrogation of the day. I've long since run out of patience, or the ability to pull my punches. "Do you have anything you'd prefer remained private?"

Delia clamps her lips shut, which I can tell is difficult for her to do. She casts a culpable look up at me with repentance in her gaze. "I see your point."

I don the my waitressing smile that has long since gone stale. "Now, then. That garden salad will be up in just a few minutes. Good to see you, Delia."

I trot to my next table, wishing I could do something to preserve Judy's dignity.

If I help solve her murder, perhaps that will help put this whole nightmare in Sweetwater Falls' rearview mirror.

9

BOOKED AND BOOKIE

"Three-hundred-eighty-four cupcakes," I announce, sucking in a long breath.

Marianne looks ready for sleep. Being that it's nearing on eleven o'clock, I am certain the bags under her eyes are a reflection of my own. "That's two dozen more than Monday's orders." She has taken it upon herself to be the bookkeeper. Thank goodness for that.

"I love that you write down how many we sell each time."

"And which flavors, and to whom they go." Marianne sets down her pen while I box up the next dozen, and then label it to go to Henry. "I think we should start a follow-up thing. The submission form on the website tracks their email address. We can send out reminders if they haven't ordered in a while. We can also send out an alert, notifying them of the flavor of the month."

I open up the next pink box and set the cupcakes inside, careful not to smear any of the frosting. "I mean, they can just check the website. I put pumpkin spice as one of the available flavors there two days ago."

"Sure, but they might not always check the website. A once-a-month email to entice them might be a good idea."

I nod, but I cannot imagine adding one more thing to my plate. "That's a good idea, but it might have to wait until I'm not working two jobs. I'm barely awake as it is. Logan's taking me out tomorrow night, and I'm worried I might fall asleep the second the lights dim at the movie theater."

Marianne yawns. "I know the feeling. But once this is your only job, you won't be this sleepy. You won't have to wait until you get off work to start baking." She jots something else in the ledger she keeps for me. "Until then, I can send out the newsletter for you."

I quirk my brow at her. "Do you know how to do that?"

Marianne snickers. "No, but neither do you. And it was my idea, so I'll take on the headache of figuring that out. I've got your passcode and username to the website in the ledger here, so I'll work on that tomorrow."

I take in her diligence, knowing there is no chance I would ever have come this far without her. "What would I do without you?" Marianne grins, but I dig deeper. "Seriously. I'm so underwater with this whole thing. You and the Live Forever Club think of all the details and then you work to make them happen. I know why other people don't have the wherewithal to follow their dreams; they don't have you."

Marianne smiles, waving away my sincerity. "This is fun for me. Are you kidding? Constant organization? It's a librarian's dream. Plus, you let me keep the books. It's a real boon to my ego." She turns her head toward the sink, her happy mood vanishing. "I sure miss our dishwasher, though. Bummer that Logan had to work late today. I can tell Judy's case is really irking him."

I fold the lid down on the box and seal it shut with a sticker that has my logo on it. "I know. I feel awful that there's not more I can do to help."

Marianne has a guilty look about her and begins fidgeting with the corner of the page. "I mean, I can think of something that *might* be helpful."

My hands slow as I take in her discomfort. "What's that?"

"We could call the bookie, you know. We could ask how much Judy's outstanding bill was. Maybe we could put the price of the cupcake order she placed towards it. I can't imagine it will even leave a dent, but it might be a nice gesture—paying down her debt."

I mull over Marianne's suggestion. "But Judy ordered cupcakes. She was celebrating. She probably won big and didn't have any debt left to pay him."

Marianne shrugs. "Maybe. But isn't it worth figuring out? Then we can cross the bookie off our list of suspects for good. And I can stop worrying that Agnes is going to lose big on her bet and have to deal with the fallout of something grim coming her way."

I chew on my lower lip, weighing the pros and cons. "I mean, what's the harm, right? If he takes the money, then that's that. We can ask him how much more she owes him, and see if it's a number worth killing her over. I felt kind of icky keeping her money, being that I can't exactly make her cupcakes."

Marianne nods. "But if he doesn't take it, then she doesn't owe him anything. Which means it wasn't him who killed her."

"One problem," I remind her. "I gave the guy's number to Logan. I don't have it anymore."

Marianne grins at me. "But we know someone who does." She picks up her phone and places a call to Agnes, who promptly gives Marianne the information we need. "See? Simple."

Without waiting for me to gather my bearings, Marianne punches in the digits, calling the bookie without more than a slip of a plan. "Hello, uh, Bookie?" She grimaces, knowing how childish we sound. "Hi, I'm calling on behalf of Judy. She placed a few bets with you recently, and I was calling to check on her account."

Marianne puts the phone on speaker so I can hear the man's voice crackling through the kitchen. "Who is this?"

"This is Judy's friend. I don't know if you heard, but she passed away recently. I found your number and wanted to see where she stood with you."

I know exactly why the Live Forever Club dubbed my best friend as Marianne the Wild. Her voice isn't even shaking.

Yet I am so nervous, I can hear my pulse in my ears.

"Oh, I didn't know she passed. I'm sorry to hear that."

"Thank you."

I can hear what sounds like him opening a book. "If you're looking to collect on her winnings, she was paid out already."

"She didn't owe anything?" Marianne asks for clarification.

The man chuckles. "No. She did for a while, but then she won three thousand dollars on the game last month. Said she was closing her account. Haven't heard from her since. Though, that could be because she died."

I flinch at his crass wording.

Marianne's eyes are wide. "Okay, thank you." She ends the call, rising from her seat. "Judy didn't owe him anything."

"And she closed her account with him, so he didn't have a reason to come after her for unpaid debts."

Marianne starts pacing back and forth across the kitchen floor. "You know what this means, right? It wasn't a suicide, and it wasn't the bookie."

My jaw tightens. "We have no suspects. This isn't good news."

Marianne points at me. "But we have Frank, whom Judy

owed a hundred dollars. That's what you said Delia told you when she was eating at the diner this morning, right?"

There isn't a thing I don't share with Marianne when we are baking together, so of course that tidbit came up while we were frosting the hundreds of cupcakes. Still, I don't like how that sounds. "Frank isn't a murderer," I insist.

Marianne's hands move to her hips. "Hey, no bad ideas in brainstorming, right?"

"I guess not, but can you picture Frank getting violent? I can barely picture him raising his voice."

Marianne shrugs. "Money brings out the worst in people." Marianne softens at my discomfort. "Hey, once we cross Frank off the list of suspects, we'll both feel a whole lot better. He's the only lead we have to go on, so I say we take it."

I peel off one of my logo stickers to place on the next box. "I mean, I was planning on walking by there tomorrow to see if Logan left me another love note."

Marianne's demeanor shifts from sleuth on a mission to poet. "I love that you two do that. It's epic, I hope you know."

Epic, yes. Wonderful, of course. But going to Frank's news-stand for a sweet letter from Logan is one thing.

Digging for dirt on Judy's murder is quite another.

FRANK'S NIECE

*M*y feet are positively dragging when my shift ends on Friday. Apparently, the closer it gets to Halloween, Bill requires the waitstaff to greet everyone with a cheery, "Happy Halloween, what can I get you to drink?" I didn't think I could loathe this job more, but that certainly tips it.

Aunt Winifred and Marianne weren't kidding when they said Sweetwater Falls gets into Halloween. On my way to work this morning, the sun wasn't awake, but I could still make out the shapes of giant pumpkins, spiders, ghouls and witches littering the sidewalk and storefronts.

Now that my shift is over and daylight illuminates the streets, I can see just how hard everyone in this town has been working on making their store the spookiest. I never cared much for scary decorations when I was a kid; I was only in it for the candy. But looking at the families of witches with warty, hooked noses hovered around the cauldrons that burble with... I'm guessing a fog machine inside; I can tell this town loves its autumn holiday.

The Nosy Newsy doesn't stay open in the evening, so I do my best attempt at a trot when I spot his business and pull over to park. My toes groan from being on my feet all day, but I ignore them. The intrigue of a note from Logan is far more pressing than physical discomfort.

Plus the prospect of questioning Frank is something I would like behind me, instead of looming over my head.

"Hi, Frank," I greet him with as much cheer as I can muster.

Frank smiles at me, revealing his missing front tooth. He jerks his thumb toward the flower box near the checkout area. "A little birdie dropped something in the flowers for you this morning on his way to work."

I practically skip to the flower box, not the least bit embarrassed that Frank knows about the love notes. I tuck the envelope into my pocket, not wanting any witnesses around to take note of my blush. "Tonight is your poker game, right?" I ask. "Logan mentioned something about it."

Frank straightens a few of the magazines on the shelf, then flicks back a piece of his greasy black hair that strayed to his forehead. "Once a month at my place. Just a handful of friends talking smack over quarters."

I don't know how to do this—how to pry circuitously without seeming obvious. "Anyone ever win big over there?"

Frank chortles. "Hard to win big when you're playing for quarters. It's more for the company than the money. Though don't you be fooled by Logan's innocent boy next door demeanor. He's ruthless when it comes to cards. Fantastic bluffer, that one."

"I'll keep that in mind." Marianne would be better at working this naturally into a conversation, but I didn't come here to chicken out. Even if I make a fool of myself, I need to rule Frank off the list of suspects. "Say, Frank? Can I ask you something?"

"Fire away, new girl."

I suck in a deep breath. "It's about Judy."

Frank's bubbly disposition sinks. "Sure. You doing okay? I can't imagine it would be easy, being the one who found her like that."

"I'm okay. Thanks for asking." I chew on my lower lip before voicing my findings. "Delia stopped by the diner this week. I heard that Judy asked you if she could borrow a hundred dollars."

Frank stiffens. "My little niece threw a fit when she found out. Did she tell you? That was private information."

I shoot him a wry look. "Heard it from Delia, who had no qualms telling me and who knows who else."

Frank closes his eyes briefly. "Ah."

"Who's your niece? Why would she care that you loaned Judy a hundred dollars?"

Frank tilts his head to the side. "Because she worked with Judy, and she's always got something to say about her."

"Huh? Who?"

"Heather. My niece. The hostess at the diner where you work."

My mouth pops open. "I had no idea you two were related."

Frank grins at me, showing off his missing front tooth. "She doesn't like to brag that she's got such a cool uncle."

I smirk his way. "I'm sure that's it. Heather didn't like that Judy borrowed money from you?"

"No, but Heather's always moody about something or another. Judy told her to thank me again for the money, and Heather wasn't too pleased."

"Wasn't pleased that you loan out money in general, or wasn't pleased that you loaned money to her coworker?"

Frank shrugs noncommittally. "No idea. She's always upset about something. You know how teenagers are."

"I guess. Heather and I don't really talk much."

Frank spreads out his hands. "Teenagers. I'm telling you,

they're the cause of every ulcer. So I gave Judy some money. What of it? Judy was in a bind, so I gave her a hundred dollars. I don't believe in loans. Told her if she wanted to 'give' me a hundred dollars one day when she was back on her feet, I wouldn't say no. But that's the end of it. I told Heather as much."

Gosh, what a nice guy. "That was sweet of you. Did Judy ever end up paying you back?"

Frank shakes his head. "No, because it wasn't a loan. She didn't give me a hundred dollars, though, no. She was a little busy being dead to bother with that. But I didn't expect it back."

"Most people would."

Frank quirks an eyebrow at me. "Not the people I hang out with. Judy was good people. I felt a little guilty. I mean, I introduced her to the bookie, and she got in over her head. If a hundred dollars can set things right for a friend, then I'm happy to give it."

My mouth pulls to the side. I want to know if he might be the type to get frustrated if Judy came into a windfall of cash and failed to give him back the hundred dollars. "I spoke to the bookie, you know." I sort through my words before speaking them. "Judy actually won quite a bit before she died."

Frank smiles—a genuine expression of happiness over something good happening to someone he liked. "You don't say. I hope she got to buy herself something irresponsible. It would be a shame if she died without being able to touch any of her winnings."

My shoulders lose their tension. "Actually, she placed an order for a dozen cupcakes. But since I didn't fill the order, I have her money and I can't return it." I open up my purse. "It's not a hundred dollars—not even close." I take out the bills and round up, so Frank doesn't have to make change. "This is from Judy. To you," I tell him, setting the money in his palm.

Frank frowns at the bills. "She didn't owe me anything. I told you, new girl. I don't loan people money. That hundred was a gift."

I smile at him, letting the best parts of Sweetwater Falls fill my spirit as I mentally cross Frank off my list of suspects. "Then consider this a gift from Judy for being such a good friend and helping her when she was in a bind."

Frank examines the bills with emotion rising in his eyes. His fingers curl around the money as his lashes sweep shut. "That, I'll accept. Thanks, new girl." Then he does something surprising and pulls me in for a hug. "You're starting to look like you belong here with us."

I sink into Frank's embrace, wondering if there was ever a sweeter compliment one could give.

RUNAWAY ARACHNID

*M*arianne points to a spot far higher than I can stretch on the outside of the library. Even perched atop the ladder as I am, I am nowhere near the hook she indicates. "I don't think I can reach it!" The wind whips at my jeans and t-shirt, reminding me that it's been quite some time since I've had good reason to climb a ladder.

Though, I'm not sure this qualifies as a good reason.

Marianne holds the base of the ladder steady for me. "I swear that's where the spider web started last year. Are you sure you can't hook it up there?"

I stretch out my arm as high as it can go, but it's not even close. "I need a stiffer rope. Or a stick. Do you see a branch anywhere you can hand me?"

Marianne releases the ladder and darts toward one of the nearby trees, fishing around on the grass until she finds something sturdy and long. "Will this work?"

"One way to find out." I hold onto the ledge of the library's tallest stained-glass window to steady myself. The breeze is doing me no favors, picking up while I am so precariously perched. My hair is in a ponytail, but the curls blow to the side, reminding me that I, too, am capable of being swayed by the wind. The days are getting shorter, which means that when the clouds roll in overhead, it's hard to tell if it's nightfall already, or if we are about to be visited by a storm.

I really don't want to be rained on while I am at the top of a metal ladder.

The things I do for Sweetwater Falls.

Really, it's what I do for Marianne. She mentioned on the phone that she was going to hang up the library's Halloween decorations after she closed for the night, and I volunteered to help without asking what that might entail.

"You really did all of this by yourself last year?" I call down to her. The ladder quakes as she moves up the rungs to hand me the branch.

"Agnes helped a bit, but ladders aren't really her thing, and heights aren't exactly my favorite. I got a high school kid to help with that part. Most of my decorations have a ladder involved."

"I see. Ambitious, are we?"

Marianne grins without a hint of her meekness in sight. "Oh, yes. The library is one of the tallest buildings in the area. Can't waste the opportunity to really do things up right."

I grip the branch and hook the top loop of the thick, cottony spiderweb over one of the notches in the wood. Holding onto the ledge of the top of the stained-glass window, I stretch as gracefully as the wind will allow, elongating my torso until the spiderweb loop finally catches on the hook three feet above my head. "I did it!"

Marianne claps her hands, which means no one is holding onto the ladder. The whole thing vibrates when a sudden gust of wind crashes into it from the side.

All of a sudden, raindrops fall fat and hard, as if someone has pierced a hole in one of the gray clouds.

We both shriek as terror slices through my façade of bravery.

I take one step down, clinging to the metal frame with all my might. What was seconds ago an unsteady surface is now slick on top of wobbly. I hug the top step as the wind slaps me on the back.

Marianne calls up to me, urging me to put one foot behind the other until I am on sturdy ground.

If only my feet wanted to move. Seconds tick by while I whimper and hold tight to the ladder. My muscles refuse to unlock until Marianne shrieks when the wind catches one of her decorations and whips it out of her hands. I can't move for my own safety, but apparently if Marianne is the least bit put out, I can do just about anything.

I nearly collapse when my feet hit the grass. My legs are rubbery, but I manage to chase after the giant spider. It looks like it's crawling as its legs drag along the slippery grass. Its body is hollow, and the whole thing is lightweight, so the wind has no trouble carrying the thing into the parking lot.

Marianne and I shriek as we chase after the enormous arachnid, not stopping until we each grab a leg to stop its flight.

My chest heaves, constricting after the fear of falling off a ladder gave way to a high-speed monster chase.

Marianne locks eyes with me, equal parts frightened and amused at the twist our evening has taken. "Are you okay?" she asks above the wave of rain that is now determined there won't be an inch of dry land anywhere in Sweetwater Falls.

I mean to answer her, but a hysterical barking laugh erupts out of my mouth. "We hunted down a twenty-five-foot-tall spider!"

Marianne's caution gives way to a grin. "Let's tie this thing down before it gets another idea in its head and takes off on us."

I reach out and pet the hairy black spider's head. "Oh, Fred. We've got you now. To the library with you."

Marianne can't stop giggling. I can't tell if her face is streaked with tears, rain, or a combination of both as we wrangle the spider back to its web.

"The legs each hook on, but we have to tie the ends of the web down first." Marianne points to a lamppost. "One end goes here. Hold onto Fred!"

I do my best, using my bodyweight to anchor the enormous spider when the wind decides it wants the thing to fly.

Marianne shrieks as she runs through the rain to the tree, tying the end of the web to a sturdy branch. She darts around the library's walkway, securing the ends the way she wants them while the wind makes a mockery of us both.

I am soaked to the skin as the curtain of rain thickens. I see Marianne darting to and fro, but it's hard to make out her shape. When she finally makes her way to me, she is panting. I'll bet her glasses are completely useless; the rain is so dense.

"We have to secure the legs now. There's a clamp under each arm." She holds up one of the legs, showing me how to be useful so we can get the job done and get out of here.

I can tell Marianne wants the spider higher up, but there is no way I am getting on that ladder a second time. We do our best, making sure we never have to go spider hunting in the rain again.

After she helps me carry the ladder to the storage area behind the library, I expect her to hug me goodbye before we run to our separate cars to part for the night. Instead, Marianne motions for me to come with her into the library. "Here. We can do the indoor stuff now."

I follow her, dumbfounded at her commitment to a children's holiday. "Are you serious?" I ask her when we stumble inside. "We're soaked!"

Marianne laughs as if this is all a great game she has been looking forward to all year. "I know, right? Now I feel like we really earned it. Everyone expects the big spider, sure, but this year, I want to take it to the next level."

"What is more formidable than a twenty-five-foot-tall spider?"

Marianne's eyebrows dance with mischief. "A spider making a home for its hundreds of babies."

I grimace at the macabre imagery. "I almost don't want to know what that entails. But I have a feeling I'm about to find out."

Marianne tugs a box out of the backroom. "These little guys have long, clear strings hanging down. When the faintest breeze catches them, they start to dance, crawling up and down the strands."

I blanche, my tongue hanging out as I take one of the spiders she hands me from the box. "Gross. You're so sweet; I never expected this from you. Oh! Oh, it's slimy!"

Marianne grins, moving to the doorway. "This is where most of them should go, but there should also be some on every shelf."

My shoulders lower. "Um, how long are you expecting to stay here tonight?"

"Oh, I don't know. It took me all night last year, but there's two of us, so it shouldn't take long at all."

I am doubtful when I see the scope of just how many spiders are in each box, but Marianne is so chipper about the chore that I don't want to rain on her already drenched parade. Besides, she has spent so many evenings helping me in the kitchen. Helping her decorate her workplace for the holiday seems like the very least I should do.

"Any word from Logan on Judy's case?" Marianne asks me as we start hanging spiders here and there. Well, *I* am hanging them here and there; Marianne seems to have a plan dictating her movements. At least she doesn't seem all that particular in telling me where the spiders I hang should go.

"Nothing that you don't already know. I wish we had any leads to go on. If this is how helpless Logan feels at his job when stuff like this comes about, I feel sorry for him."

Marianne fishes out three more spiders with fat bodies the size of softballs, each one black and hairy. "Well, let's start from the beginning. Judy didn't hurt herself, so we can rule that out. She had money problems and started placing bets on games. She lost a lot, then borrowed money from Frank."

"Not borrowed." I remind her of Frank's phrasing which I relayed to her on the phone earlier. "Frank *gave* her the money. Didn't seem fussed at all that he might never get it back."

"What a sweetheart."

I chuckle at the correct assessment, though when I first met the man, that is not the descriptor I would have used. "So it's not Frank who was after Judy."

Marianne sighs. "I wish we hadn't turned in Judy's diary. We could give that another look to see if we find any clues in the pages."

We hang up the spiders in companionable silence while we mull over the possible leads we might have overlooked.

Marianne pauses, glancing over at me. "Hey, I know this isn't how you were hoping to spend one of your few free evenings. Thanks for helping."

"I was hoping to spend the evening with you, so I'm living my best life. Never thought I would say that so close to a box of spiders, but life is full of surprises."

Marianne's pep takes a dive, her shoulders lowering. "Today would have been my anniversary with my ex-fiancé. Not of when Jeremy proposed, but when we first started dating. I could have probably picked a less rainy night to hang up the outdoor decorations, but I really didn't want to be alone tonight. I do better with grief when I keep myself busy."

Marianne doesn't often bring up the sore spot of her engagement gone awry. I treat the topic tenderly. "Oh, honey. I didn't realize. Jeremy is such a fool. Cheating on someone as amazing as you?" I shake my head at the whole mess. I never met the idiot who left his high school sweetheart for someone else, but I know that if I did, I would have some choice words for the lowlife. "It's good that we did the decorations tonight, then. That was smart thinking. And after we finish here, I think we deserve a slumber party. Feel like cookie dough and popcorn?"

Marianne perks up. "Really? You don't have to. I know you're tired."

She's not wrong, but there is nowhere I would rather be than with her, especially when she's feeling down. "I think you need to spend the night tonight. I mean, we have to keep up your donut on a string training. We shaved four seconds off your record yesterday. If we keep at it, you'll be the donut champion at the festival."

Marianne drops her macabre decorations and crosses the room, engulfing me in a giant hug. "Thank you. I don't want to be alone tonight."

I squeeze her harder. "Don't you know? A best friend makes sure that you never have to be alone. Just say the word, okay?"

Marianne releases me with moisture glistening in her eyes. "Back to work, then?"

"Absolutely."

We keep at our job in companionable silence for a few minutes while my mind drifts back to Judy and the unsolvable riddle of her death. I know there is something I am missing, so I dig deep into my memory to pull out anything of import.

"Sally!" I blurt out when the conversation with Delia at the diner comes back to me. Working two jobs and spending my free evenings fending off a panic attack atop a ladder is starting to mess with my recall. "Do you know who Sally is?"

Marianne shrugs. "Sure. I mean, we're not close friends, but everyone in Sweetwater Falls knows everyone to some extent. What about her?"

"Well, I talked to Frank about the money Judy borrowed because Delia told me about it. But she mentioned another person Judy borrowed money from. What do you know about Sally?"

Marianne's mouth pulls to the side. "Not much. She's a hairdresser. Owns the salon in town." Marianne grabs an armload of furry spiders and hangs them around the circulation desk. She squeezes one affectionately. "I love these little guys. When you turn the switch on their bellies, they make a creepy scuttling sound."

I blanche. "I don't think I'm cut out for Sweetwater Falls' version of Halloween. I grew up on caramel-dipped apples and pumpkin painting."

Marianne quirks an eyebrow at me. "Like, scary pumpkin painting?"

I shake my head. "My pumpkins were fairy princesses."

"Scary princesses?"

I chuckle at Marianne's totally wrong guess. "These spiders are creeping me out."

Marianne grins at me. "That's the idea." Then she flexes her meager muscle. "Don't worry; I'll protect you."

I clasp my hands under my chin. "My hero!" I grimace when one of the spiders makes a slurping squishing sound the moment I pick it up. "Hairdresser, eh? You know, funny thing about working two jobs. I haven't had a minute to get my hair trimmed. I might need to stop by and book an appointment with Sally."

Marianne grins at my train of thought. "What a wonderful idea. I might need a trim, too. It's been a while."

I love that Marianne is just as into getting to the bottom of this as I am. In fact, there's not much about my best friend that I don't love. Even her affection for creepy Halloween items is endearing. Marianne the Wild, indeed.

Marianne goes online and books two appointments for us, requesting Sally so we get double the amount of time to sneak in our questions.

One way or another, we will get to the bottom of Judy's murder.

And we'll have fabulous hair while we do it.

SALLY'S BEAUTY BARN

J am not what you would call an adventurous person. Opening up my cupcake business took a fair amount of Marianne holding my hand, and Lisa Swanson drawing up a detailed step-by-step plan of how to reach my goal. When I sit down in Sally's salon chair, I haven't contemplated anything more than a half-inch trim to keep my blonde waves from frizzing at the ends.

Sally's Beauty Barn is exactly as small town as I expected it to be. There are a few women with big hair teased to the heavens who are giving their clients a similar look. There are pink lacy curtains around the windows, and everything inside has the feel of a Southern Belle's salon to it. Instead of magazines, there are Amish romance novels strewn on the table in the waiting area.

It's kind of adorable.

There's even an orange tabby cat who bats around a jingly pink, glittery ball.

Marianne picks up the cat, stroking its fur while she frowns. "I haven't had my hair cut in ages at a salon. I usually trim it myself."

"Getting cold feet?" I ask her when a woman calls my name.

I glance up at the forty-something woman with tall, teased brown hair. "That's me. Are you Sally?"

"Sure am, kitten. Come on over and take a load off." She pats the back of her salon chair, smiling brightly at me. "You're the new girl, right? Winifred's niece? I've heard all about you. Winifred was so excited to have you come live with her. Told everyone for a solid week all about you. Even showed me your picture. She told us you looked like an angel atop a Christmas tree, and was she ever right. I love this hair, honey. I can tell it hasn't been processed all that much." She fluffs my hair and fans the bib around my neck before she starts combing out my curls. "Are you in the mood for some highlights? Fancy being a redhead?"

"Um, I..."

"Oh, you probably want to keep this hair as it is. Just a trim?"

"Yeah, so..."

"Sounds great. Oh, honey. Let me tell you about the time..."

And that's how most of the appointment goes. Each time Sally asks a question, she answers it herself. She talks a mile a minute, so much that if I speak more than a word or two, I feel rude for interrupting her.

By the time my haircut is finished, I haven't managed more than a half sentence at a time.

I need to get better at being direct. I came here with a list of questions to ask Sally, but I haven't managed a single one.

With my tail between my legs, I hand the chair off to Marianne.

My best friend stands, determination in her eyes and fire in her steps as she stalks over to Sally and sits down with authority. "I want you to chop my hair to my chin. Shorter, even."

Sally's mouth falls open in time with my own. "Are you sure, kitten? That's a big change."

"I'm not sure, but let's do it anyway." Marianne's teeth worry her lower lip. She locks her gaze onto mine. "I need a change. I want to do something wild."

Sally's caution is not the expression the Live Forever Club would have. I pull out my phone and call Winifred while Sally undoes Marianne's two long brown braids, letting the crimped hair fall to the middle of her back. I'm not sure I've ever seen Marianne with her hair down. I love her pretty hair. I snap a picture to send to Carlos.

"Aunt Winnie? Grab the girls and get to Sally's Beauty Barn. Marianne the Wild is about to show her true colors."

That's all Aunt Winnie needs to hear. When I end the call, I tune into Marianne's firm hold on the conversation. "Judy mentioned how good you are at cutting hair. Did you do hers?"

Sally takes her time combing out Marianne's tresses. I can tell she's been spooked into near silence, contemplating how to go about cutting off such pretty hair to such a drastic cut. "Only for fun. Judy used to let me practice on her back in the day before I got my hairdresser license. Shame what happened to her."

Marianne swallows hard but doesn't hold back. "Delia mentioned that you loaned Judy fifty bucks before she passed. That was nice of you."

Sally stills, frowning. "Delia's got a big mouth. Judy is my friend. She needed fifty bucks, so I gave it to her. She helped me out when I needed someone to experiment on when I was learning how to color and cut hair. She watches my cat for me when I'm out of town and never asks for a dime."

Marianne doesn't shrink but smiles at Sally. "Sounds like you two were close."

"We were closer years ago, but we keep in touch still. We've had enough good moments that I don't loan her anything. She needed fifty dollars, so I gave it to her. I owe her a lot more than that for how much she's helped me out over the years. Do you know how expensive it is to board your cat at a kennel?"

"No idea. I'm glad you two had each other. I'm so sorry she's gone."

Sally nods as a tear falls down her plump cheek. "I'm sorry. I need to take a break for a minute. I'll be right back."

Marianne and I share matching looks of horror that we made a woman cry. Marianne makes to move, but she's wearing a giant salon bib, so I wave for her to sit down as I dart into the backroom for employees.

While the front of the salon is decorated for customers, the breakroom has a muted quality to it, with bare walls and a table overflowing with clutter.

My hand moves to my sternum. "Sally, you poor thing. We shouldn't have made you talk about any of this. I didn't realize you were close to Judy. We're trying to learn more about her."

Sally sits at a table and chairs, snatching at a box of crackers atop the table. "Judy kept to herself. We were closer before her mother died. After that, she preferred to keep to herself. I should have pushed harder. I should have made her get out of the house and do things. Months of that turned into years. I still talked to her. Called on her when I needed help or when a big moment in my life happened. I should have pushed my way into the house with her and sat with her in the sadness."

Sally casts around for a tissue, so I grab the box nearest to me and sit down with her, plucking out a few to hand over. "You did what you thought she needed. Sometimes people need space and prefer to grieve alone."

"Yeah, but then Judy started to *be* alone. I didn't want that. I feel awful about this whole thing. There's so much guilt swimming around inside of me that I can barely think about Judy without hating myself."

My thoughts immediately go to Marianne. If she hadn't

reached out last night and asked me to be with her on what she knew would be a hard day for her (even though she didn't tell me why until halfway through the evening), she would have spent a truly difficult day alone. I don't want to picture my best friend holed up in her home, all alone because she is too depressed to muscle up the strength to invite someone in. I couldn't bear it. I wouldn't be able to stand not knowing her.

I reach across the table and hold Sally's hand, squeezing her fingers until she squeezes back. I want this woman not to have to cry alone. Though I don't know her at all, no one should have to muscle through grief in a poorly lit breakroom, crying over a box of stale crackers.

I stay with Sally, offering gentle words whenever she will hear them. I hold her hand until her tears dry.

"Thank you," Sally says to me. "I'm sorry I'm falling apart like this. You came in for a haircut, not a therapy session."

Actually, I came in to ask questions about Judy, no matter how uncomfortable.

But I don't say that. Instead, I stand with her and offer her a hug. "Any time, you hear me? Whenever you feel sad about Judy, I want you to reach out. Here's my number." I let go of her and scribble my phone number on tissue that I hand her. "Judy was grieving, so she isolated herself, it sounds like. Let's not let that happen again, okay? Are you going to the Halloween Festival?"

Sally casts me a watery smile. "I am. And you're right. I have friends. I don't know why I'm not talking to them about this. It's all bottling up until it explodes on my poor, unsuspecting customers." She shakes her head, her mouth turning stern. "Delia shouldn't be spreading around Judy's business. So what if Judy needed fifty bucks? We all have times like that. It doesn't do anyone a lick of good if we use other people's down moments as fodder for town gossip."

"Agreed. You're a good friend. If I hear anything more about that, I'll shut down the talk right away." I take a tissue and dab under Sally's eyes to stop the streaking of her mascara. "I'm going to the Halloween Festival, too. I'll see you there, okay? And when I see you, I'm buying you a drink."

Sally smiles at me. "Deal. The Live Forever Club makes wink-wink cider. That's my drink of choice."

I chuckle at my aunt's antics. Her wink-wink lemonade for adults only at the Lemonade Festival this summer was a big hit with the fairgoers.

Sally and I walk out of the breakroom together just as the Live Forever Club enters the salon.

Marianne looks horrified that she made Sally cry. She can't stop apologizing until Agnes asks where Marianne the Wild has gone.

Marianne chews on her lower lip. "I was thinking it's time for a change. I've been wearing my hair the exact same way since I was a little girl. Yesterday was a hard day for me. Really put things into perspective."

Agnes closes her eyes and hisses. I can tell she is mentally kicking herself for forgetting the important date. "Oh, honey. Please tell me you didn't sit home alone."

Marianne shakes her head while Sally recombs the left side. "I had my best friend with me."

I posture, grateful to be a person anyone calls on when they are in need of emotional support. "Tell them what you were thinking for your hair."

Marianne touches the middle of her cheek with the side of her hand.

It's not easy to shock the three members of the Live Forever Club, but that sure does the trick. Karen, Agnes and Aunt Winnie all widen their eyes, their mouths falling open.

Agnes takes hold of Marianne's right hand and Karen grips Marianne's left. Karen nods to Sally with all the determination of one commanding a ship's crew. "Go on, then. Marianne the Wild has worlds to conquer."

I watch with my hands covering my silent scream as Sally takes her scissors and chops off an entire foot of Marianne's beautiful hair.

13

THE JUDY SPECIAL

*N*ot to be dramatic, but today is the ten millionth day I have waited tables at the diner, and it's about the fifteenth time this morning that I have had to tell someone that broccoli and cheese is our soup of the day.

The soup of the day never changes. Every day is broccoli and cheese soup day. The broth tastes like burnt rubber, and the broccoli bears no resemblance to its namesake. It's basically a yellow soup so thick, your spoon stands up in it, and it's littered with green confetti. I've never seen a broccoli chunk in there to speak of.

Still, people come in asking what the soup of the day might be, even though it has never changed.

When I go to put in the order for two tables I've just waited on, Bill claps me on the shoulder. He loves when the diner is full. "Hey, push the new soup, will you?"

I blink at him. "There's a new soup?"

Bill beams at me. "Yep. Just came up with it yesterday. It's the Judy Special. Broccoli and cheese soup with a buttered roll."

I cringe at everything he just said. "So, the soup of the day, but with a buttered roll instead of crackers?"

"Yep. I tried it out in my section over there, and it sold like gangbusters."

I set my hand on my hip. "Did Judy ever once order broccoli and cheese soup?"

He shrugs. "I'm sure she did at one point or another. It's the only soup on the menu. I have it every day."

I fight the urge to raise my voice. "Making money off of someone's memory is disgusting. In no way will I tell my tables that there is a Judy Special."

Bill grumbles at me, but then turns to the diner at large. He puts two fingers to his lips and delivers an ear-piercing whistle that makes me and several others wince. "In honor of our deceased waitress, we are now offering the Judy Special: a bowl of broccoli and cheese soup with a buttered roll. Judy's favorite."

I guffaw at his gall, but several people in my section raise their hands, indicating that they would like that added to their order.

Gross. If I ever die and someone names this horrible soup after me, I will do some serious haunting of the offender.

I go about my shift with a significant chip on my shoulder, though I try not to let my customers bear the brunt of my stewing. Each time someone orders the Judy Special, I begin to lose my faith in humanity.

That is, until I go to bus a table an hour later.

I am surprised to find two twenties left for my tip. I frown at the money, guessing this was left by mistake. The older couple's bill came to fifteen dollars and some change. I'm not a terrible waitress, but I'm not so good that I deserve more than a hundred percent tip.

"Excuse me!" I call to the people who are putting on their jackets as they slip out the front door. "Excuse me, I think you left this by mistake," I say to them as I trot out into the chilly autumn air without a coat. I shiver as I hand them back their bills. "You probably meant to put down two singles. I didn't want you to get home and realize your mistake too late."

The older man smiles at me while his wife takes my hand and folds my fingers over the bills. "That's for you, young lady. The least we could do."

My nose crinkles. "What do you mean?"

The man casts a culpable look at his wife before he answers. "We used to sit in Judy's section before she..." He allows decorum and silence finish the sentence before he continues. "We heard that she was in need of money, and that might have been the reason she..." Again comes the silence that assumes Judy killed herself instead of being murdered. "We're always fifteen percent tippers. Maybe if we had rounded up to twenty percent, Judy would still be alive."

The old woman pats my hand. "You're doing a great job in there, sweetheart. Keep it and have a good day."

My mouth is dry. "Who told you that Judy needed money?"

"Oh, we heard it from Delia, who heard it from someone. You know how things spread. We don't want anyone to go through that. Poor dear. Judy was a good girl." The woman's eyes moisten. "I was knitting a scarf for her. I finished it, too. Now I don't know what to do with it." When she takes in my shiver, she lights up. "You should have it! I'll bring it by later today. Oh, that solves it. I've been staring at this scarf for weeks now, trying to figure out who should have it."

My mouth falls open at the generosity. "You really don't have to."

She pinches my cheek as if she has known me long enough to do that. Because she is sweet and older, I let her. "Oh, humor me. It'll make me feel better, knowing someone will use it." She grips my hand. "Say, do you happen to know if anyone ever checked on Judy's cat?"

I still. "What?"

"Judy's cat, Whiskers. Any idea if it's in need of a new home? I'd hate to think of the poor dear being sent to a pound. It's an outdoor cat, which we wouldn't mind at all."

"I'll ask."

"Thank you. I'm Nancy, and this is Nick. He plays Santa Claus at the Christmas Festival every year," she brags, clearly proud of her husband. He actually does look like he could play the role of Santa Claus, what with his white hair, beard and bulbous belly.

Gosh, they're cute. "I'm Charlotte McKay."

"Oh, we know. You're Winifred's niece. The cupcake baker. Say, do you happen to cater parties? It's a bit early, but we always host a dinner in December for our friends. Last year, we had thirty people! Is that the sort of thing you do? I usually make the desserts, but I think I deserve a year off from all the work in the kitchen."

I light up. "Absolutely!" I jot down my website for them on a scrap piece of paper. I resist the urge to hug the woman, but when she opens her arms, I jump right on in. "It was nice to meet you. And thank you for the generous tip. Truly."

"Go on, dear. I'll be back in a bit with that scarf. You're going to freeze over if we keep you out here a second longer."

The two send me on my way back to the diner with a lot to think about. Though I am not supposed to use my cell phone during my shift, I pull it out and text Logan, asking him if anybody located Judy's cat.

When Logan responds a minute later with a frown emoji next to "Judy had a cat? Are you sure?" my stomach sinks.

Poor baby. Bill barks at me to get off my phone, but as he ignored my chiding on the cross addition of the Judy Special, I feel little guilt in texting Marianne, asking her if she wants to look for Whiskers at Judy's house when I get off my shift and she finishes hers.

I feel terrible that I knew nothing about Judy, and hope we are not too late to save her cat.

14

YARDWORK AND CAT HUNT

Though we have Logan with us, the worry that we are breaking and entering haunts me more than it should. I'm not even inside of Judy's house. Logan has his uniform and badge, which is all the permission we need. He lets himself inside to search for the cat while Marianne and I scour the property around her home.

"Here, Whiskers!" Marianne coos in a high-pitched voice. "Here, baby!" She thinks of everything, including bringing along a tin of wet cat food to coerce Whiskers out of her hiding place. "Here, kitty-kitty!"

I never had a pet growing up, which is just as well. I'm better with pets like fish, who require little more than being fed once a day, along with the occasional change of water. Though, if I was being honest, cuddling up to a cat in the evening is a nice visual.

"Whiskers!" I call gently, trying to keep my voice as singsong as Marianne's. She is a natural with anything that requires gentility or kindness.

There are two tall trees on Judy's property. The one in the front yard has a trunk so thick, I can't wrap my arms around it. It stretches skyward, its leaves a pretty golden red.

Though it's hardly Judy's fault that the yard hasn't been raked, it is clear to me that the state of disrepair her yard fell into happened long before her passing. Thick branches have taken up residence on the lawn, which is now littered with fallen leaves. The grass is overgrown, which is to be expected, but there are divots in the grass which make me think Judy had a mole or groundhog that decided to take over her landscaping duties.

The ranch-style home is small but cute. It is in need of a little care, especially when I see that the red of the brick is marred on the side of the house by a green fungus that's grown up the side.

Poor thing, I think to myself. *She must have been completely overwhelmed.* A house is a lot of work, especially when you are tight on cash and can't afford to update every now and then. I never checked on her. We rarely had more than a "Can you believe Bill today? My goodness, what a grump," sort of an exchange. I didn't sit down with her, though I had the chance. I was so busy trying to find a way to get out of that place that I forgot to look at the people around me.

I move to the one-car garage and take out a rake.

"What are you doing, Charlotte?" Marianne asks with the tin of cat food still in her hand.

"I didn't know her," I admit as if confessing to a horrid crime. "Look at this place. Judy needed help, and I had no idea." I take the rake to the corner of the yard and start sweeping the leaves into a pile. "Had I taken ten minutes to get to know her, maybe she wouldn't be..." My voice catches, but I refuse to feel sad for more than a second.

Marianne pauses her search for Whiskers to stare at me. "Charlotte, you know Judy's death isn't your fault."

I don't like arguing with Marianne, but the self-loathing spills out of my mouth while I take my frustration out on the leaves. "Selfish. All I thought about at the diner was how much I wanted not to be there. I didn't get to know her. I didn't even try. My whole focus is starting my business, so much that I've taken over your life. And Winnie's. And Karen's. And Agnes'. Even Logan!" I tear at the leaves, exerting more energy than strictly necessary, because I am so angry with myself. "I made all of you drop your plans and focus on my business. Me, me, me."

Marianne crosses the backyard to stand a few feet from me, her arms crossed over her chest. "Is that how you really see this?"

"It's how it is! I didn't notice that Judy was drowning. I didn't even know her last name!"

Marianne holds up her hand, her hip cocked to the side. I don't know what it is about her—maybe it's the new haircut—but she exudes enough command to still my rake. "First off, I know about five things more than you about Judy, and I've known her most of my life. Some people like to keep to themselves."

"Yeah, but..."

Marianne refuses to let me flog myself a second longer. "How did you spend your evening during the rainstorm? Was it baking cupcakes, which you have every right to do? No. You spent it with me, helping me with my job, pursuing my goal of having the scariest building on the block. You did it without a thought, climbed on a shaky ladder for me and reached your hand into a box of furry spiders because my needs were more important than yours that night." She motions between us. "That's how friendships work." She tosses her hand to the side. "This whole thing is horrible. Death is scary. Murder is frightening. But blaming yourself for it isn't how this works."

My shoulders lower. I don't know how I got to be an inch from tears, but I feel pressure behind my eyes building.

"And the fact that you think the Live Forever Club won't

hesitate to tell it like it is shows how turned around you are right now. Do you think Winifred, Karen and Agnes would invest the time and energy in us if we were lost causes? They do what they want, and what they want is to see us succeed."

I swallow hard as the breeze picks up around us. "She died all alone," I tell Marianne, my heart still aching, even though I am moving past the self-flagellation stage.

Marianne clears the gap between us. "Now that, you can feel sad about. Judy didn't deserve that at all."

I exhale as Marianne wraps her arms around me, centering me when my insides start to swirl.

I am about to tell her how much she means to me, but Marianne's voice hits my ears without the swell of confidence she just exuded. "I can't bake. My whole life, I watched those cooking shows and tried my hardest to get it right. I can cook just fine, but baking is different. It's science mixed with art."

I've never heard it put like that before, but she's right. If you get the science wrong, the cupcake will have the wrong consistency or will fall flat. If you forget to add some soul to the recipe, then all you have is a stupid chocolate cupcake that's utterly forgettable the second you swallow. A mouthful of sugar and nothing more.

Marianne holds me tight. "You let me mix things and learn while we work together. You didn't know I was horrible at baking, so after a while, I forgot I was bad at it. I watched you work. Over and over, you made the same cupcake recipe. I studied how many times you hand-mixed things. I watched in amazement each time you added an ingredient without measuring. If you think I come over to bake with you for purely unselfish reasons, you are wrong. I want to learn, so you teach me. Is that wrong?"

My chest quakes with happiness. "Of course not. It's smart. And you're a fantastic baker. There have been many batches that you've made entirely by yourself while I put together the frosting."

Marianne pulls back, beaming. "That never would have happened if you hadn't let me in. It's not selfish to share your passions. In fact, sharing is a selfless activity." She kisses my cheek. "So I don't want to hear anything more about what a horrible person you think you are. It's not true."

Now my cheeks are wet. I don't know how I got so lucky to stumble upon a friend like this.

I clutch the rake and start sweeping the leaves into a pile again, though this time with less antipathy in each stroke. "What sorts of desserts have you always wanted to try making? Cupcakes are my happiness, but there's a whole world of baking with which you can fall in love."

Marianne grins, now that she has effectively saved the day. "Cheesecakes. Every time I look at one of those recipes, though, I get overwhelmed and stop before I start. There are so many steps."

"The beautiful thing about baking is that if we mess up, all we've wasted is a few eggs and an hour. It's okay to get things wrong." I pause to gage how well she receives my words. "You know that, right?"

Marianne frowns as if I've told her the sky is polka dotted. "I think the point of baking is to get it right."

"Sure, but the happiest moments come from serendipitous accidents. A cheesecake that doesn't set can be a fabulous dip for fruit."

Marianne's mouth draws to the side. "I guess I never thought of it like that. I thought it was either pass or fail."

A conversation about cheesecake being a reflection on life is right up my alley. "Let's make some cheesecakes this weekend. Then we'll see how big a failure you feel you are. A few will make it; a few won't. Either way, we'll have fun while we learn what works and what doesn't."

Marianne's grin is filled with trepidation. "Really? You don't mind?"

I smile at her and continue raking. "I never mind making a mess in the kitchen."

Logan's voice floats on the breeze. "If we're taking requests, I can't bake at all, either. I tried watching while you do your thing, but you go too fast for me to keep up."

My goodness, I temporarily forgot how handsome Logan is in his uniform. The blue makes the beautiful green of his eyes stand out that much more.

Marianne grins at him. "This weekend we're making cheesecakes."

"I could stand to learn that, if you need a dishwasher."

Marianne and I nod in unison. "You know we like having you around," I add. Though the second those words hit the air, I wonder if they are too forward.

"You do?" Logan's half-smile has a tease to it. "Then would you teach me how to make peanut brittle? My grandpa loves the stuff, but when I gave it a go, I nearly cracked a tooth trying a piece."

I love that they have goals, and I get to be part of the ride. "It's been a while, but we can try that together." I love that we have plans.

Marianne gasps, though she's not looking at us any longer. "Whiskers!" she whispers, pointing to the fence. "I put the cat food down over there, and she's going for it!"

Logan's hand moves to his chest. "Thank goodness. I was bracing myself for the mental image of stumbling upon a dead cat."

Marianne holds her arms out. "Don't anyone move. Let her get used to us." She gives it a few seconds for Whiskers to start enjoying the tin of food before she inches closer, making sure to keep her movements slow and fluid.

I hold my breath without meaning to the closer she gets. I don't exhale until Marianne has Whiskers in her arms.

It is no surprise that only the gentlest of souls can comfort this poor cat who has lost her mommy. Whiskers leans into Marianne's embrace while she eats from the tin.

Logan heads to his truck and pulls out a small cage meant to transport animals. It looks so sad and cold that Marianne refuses to put her in it. "I'll just hold her on my lap."

Logan frowns. "I'm not sure that's the best idea."

"It's either that, or I walk home holding her. I don't want her to be frightened. I'm not putting her in jail, Logan."

He runs his hand over his face. "Ah, jeez. It's not jail, Marianne. It's a cage meant to keep her safe until we can get her to Nick and Nancy. You're sure they said they want to take her in?"

I nod. "They're the reason I knew Judy had a cat."

It's clear Logan doesn't like the idea of a cat in the cab of his truck, but I've yet to meet the unfeeling soul who can say no to Marianne.

"Oh, fine, but I have to stay here a little while longer. I found something inside, and I'm waiting on my partner."

My interest is piqued, even as Marianne hefts herself into the truck with Whiskers in her arms. Though I am not a cop, I follow Logan as he moves back toward the house, slipping inside with him to see what clues may have come to light.

15

BREAKING IN

*M*y footsteps are careful as I move into the small house. The first thing I notice is Logan's frown as he stands in the center of the living room, glancing at the front window. "Everything okay?" I ask Logan.

He rubs the nape of his neck. "I'm not sure. The back door was unlocked and not closed all the way. I noticed it while you two were searching outside for the cat. When we went through the house the first time, I am positive it was all locked up. Now I'm wondering what else has been messed with."

I keep my voice quiet, worried he might realize I am technically not supposed to be in here. "Did one of the officers open it to air out the house?"

"We don't do that sort of thing. Unless there is a dead body, we leave the house as we found it." He motions to the kitchen. "In there I saw splintering on the doorjamb. It definitely wasn't there when we checked the house before."

"Meaning whoever was in here Judy didn't trust enough to give them a key."

Logan taps his temple. "Exactly. There's a shoeprint on the

linoleum that wasn't there before, either. A smaller sneaker, so not something one of our guys would have worn."

I move into the kitchen, noting the few undone dishes in the sink, a grocery list on the fridge and a cat dish licked clean. My steps still when I take in the mark on the floor. "Um, I think you would have noticed that your first time through the house. An opened back door plus a mud stain this big? Logan, someone broke into Judy's house."

Logan sighs. "I think so, too. I called it in while you and Marianne were looking for the cat. Took a few pictures and sent them in.

I fight the urge to wash Judy's dishes. I'm fairly certain I am not supposed to touch stuff. "Is anything missing? Any valuables?"

Logan shrugs. "That's what I'll need Wayne's help seeing. There really aren't any valuables worth stealing."

"Are you sure about that? And even if you're right, the person breaking in didn't necessarily know that." I mill through the house, noting anything that looks out of place or hastily strewn aside. "Logan!" I call, drawing him to Judy's bedroom. It feels wrong stepping inside without her permission, so I stay in the doorway, pointing to an opened jewelry box. "Was that opened when you were here last?"

"No. I don't think so." He peers inside. "But there's still jewelry in here. We didn't do an inventory, so I can't tell if anything is missing, but if they were going to steal her jewelry, they left it all here."

I stand on my toes, peering from a distance. "All of that looks like costume jewelry, Logan. None of it is valuable."

Logan frowns into the jewelry box. "Fair point."

My mind immediately goes to the worst possible scenario. "If they didn't come here to steal, then maybe they came to clean up evidence. That's always a possibility."

Logan sighs. The sound is so dejected that I immediately forget my surroundings and move to his side. "If I wanted to hold onto my faith in humanity, maybe I should have picked a different profession."

I reach out and hold onto his hand, squeezing it so he doesn't have to feel the swings of life's lows alone.

Logan draws me into his arms, his cheek pressed to mine. We breathe together for one entire moment, ignoring the world while it does its best to prove to us that people are terrible, and there will always be murderers lurking where you least expect. My arms act as a shield, fending off the horrible things that might drag Logan away from his hard-earned optimism.

When his hand moves up and down my back, I wonder if there is a more wonderful place in all the world than remaining in his arms for however long life grants us.

It's only the opening of the front door that tears me out of his arms as if we've been caught mid-scandal.

"Wayne!" Logan's voice cracks as he greets his partner. "Thanks for coming so quick."

Wayne dips his head to me when he enters the hallway. "Ma'am. What do we have here, Logan?"

"A break-in, though I'm not sure why or who. Nothing seems to be missing."

Wayne frowns. "Maybe it's not a robbery? I mean, if nothing is missing, then it's a break-in, sure, but for what? Maybe someone wanted to feel close to Judy one last time. Maybe it's a friend who loaned her a jacket or whatever, and broke in to take it back."

"That's possible," Logan muses, though he doesn't sound convinced.

I keep my distance, remaining in the hallway while Wayne and Logan poke around Judy's bedroom. "Could be a friend, sure, but to me it seems like whoever broke in didn't find what they were looking for."

Logan inhales a long breath and then tosses me his keys. "Can you take Marianne and deliver the cat to Nick and Nancy? I might be here for a while. I'm sure Whiskers is going to get antsy, waiting for me in the car."

I sift his keys through my fingers as I walk toward the front entrance of the house, wondering who on earth might want to break into a dead woman's home, and what they could have stolen to make the crime worth the risk.

A NEW CHALLENGE

*M*aking donuts isn't all that different from cupcakes. I'm not frying them, so it's an easy effort on my part to take some of the batter, thicken it up and bake a few donuts using a pan I rarely have need to get out. While the various flavors of cheesecakes bake in the oven, Marianne sets to practicing for the big donut showdown.

Watching Marianne go at this donut, which is hung from the clothesline outside in the backyard, is the best entertainment I could ask for. With her hands dutifully behind her back, she uses teeth and tongue to munch delicately so as not to knock the dessert to the ground. It's a tenuous dance between wanting to finish quickly and not letting your donut fall to the grass, which would result in immediate disqualification during the competition.

When she finishes, I rattle off her time, noting her sloped shoulders. "Are you kidding me? How is it possible I'm getting worse at this? That's two seconds longer than yesterday."

"The new haircut might take some getting used to. I'll bet that's what is throwing you off your game." I hold up my phone, displaying the timer. "And I'm sorry, but two seconds is hardly worth kicking yourself over."

Marianne harrumphs as a bird lands on the clothesline. "I was hoping to kill it this year. I mean, really wipe the floor with everyone else. Rip always makes such a big deal over the winner. Announces their name loudly over the speaker and gives this huge speech about how donuts are like our town—sweet and without end." She waves off my confusion over anyone waxing poetic about a donut. "You have to hear it."

"I can't wait."

It's been a few days since Marianne had her hair chopped to just above her chin, but I'm still not used to it. It's adorable, to be sure, but I can't stop staring at what a difference the style has made to her whole demeanor.

"Girls?" I hear Agnes call from inside the house. "I hope you weren't planning on keeping whatever smells so good from us. We worked up a real appetite while we were out."

Just hearing a member of the Live Forever Club's voice splits my face into a grin. "Cheesecakes," I call through the open window. "They've got about five more minutes. Then they'll need taste testers."

Karen saunters out into the backyard, covered in what looks like red slime. "Perfect. That will give the desserts time to bake and cool while I rinse off. Do you mind if I borrow your bathrobe or a change of clothes, Charlotte?"

I point at her, torn between horrified and amused. "Care to explain what hijinks you've been up today?"

Karen looks down at her body while it drips red ooze onto the grass. "Oh, you know. Just getting ready for the Halloween Festival. The high schoolers always think their display is going to be scariest, but they don't know real fear." She shakes her head, her chin firming. "If they win again this year, I swear..."

"There's a spooky display contest?" I ask Marianne. Every new piece of this town that unfolds always manages to baffle me.

Marianne nods. "They're called Spook Booths. All entrants get a closed-off space about the size of your kitchen. Maybe a little bigger. Then people vote on whose display was scariest. I don't compete in that one. I like decorating the library. That's a separate category."

I chuckle at how serious they are taking this. "Wow. I had no idea anyone could care about Halloween this much. I can't wait to see it all."

My peppy statement is a partial lie. I really don't like being scared, and much prefer cute autumn decorations to the frightening ones that act as inspiration for my nightmares.

Karen winks at us. "Well, no spoilers this year. You're just going to have to be surprised like everyone else. Those teenagers won't know what hit them."

I love how seriously everyone takes this rivalry, and how silly the whole thing actually is. When I lived in the big city, there weren't festivals to see who made the scariest booth. Or, if there were, I was too shy to give any of it a chance. I'm not sure I have outgrown my tendency toward introversion and isolation, but life with these four has made it plain that I don't have much of a choice if I'm going to keep up with them.

If Judy had been granted four angels like I have now, perhaps she would still be alive.

Marianne wipes off her mouth and tilts her head to the side. "What's wrong? Your face got all serious and sad for a second. That's not a cheesecake expression."

I snort at her phrasing. "What exactly is a cheesecake expression?"

Marianne dons a wistful countenance and sighs dreamily. "Something like that. What's going on?"

I reach for another donut from the plate and take down the

end of the clothesline, so I can string the next for Marianne. "Oh, nothing. I was just thinking how lucky I am to have you all pushing me to try things I otherwise never might. I'll bet if Judy had people like you, she wouldn't have been so isolated."

Though she is still sopping with the red goo from head to toe, Karen speaks as if not a hair is out of place. "I'm glad you came to us, Charlotte McKay. And don't think for one second that Agnes and Winnie don't have to push me on occasion to step outside of my comfort zone." She motions to her wrecked attire. "Laughter is only as good as the people you share it with."

It never occurred to me that Karen, of all people, might have boundaries that need pushing. "You always seem so sure of yourself."

Karen bats at my words. "Oh, no. Sometimes, yes, I get a rush of bravery and do what I like. But without my girls, I would be indoors most days, wondering why I'm living but don't feel alive." She crosses her arms, her movement making a slurping noise. "I was thinking that it might be time for me to take a new risk."

I love that Karen says this fresh from whatever feat drove her to be covered in red slime.

Marianne stills. "Are we talking new hairstyle, or will there be bail money involved?"

Karen smiles at Marianne's new hairdo. "I think you took the lead in new hairstyles." Karen motions to me. "Winnie took in Charlotte. Agnes took you under her wing, Marianne. I like my privacy, but maybe I need to push myself. I don't want to wake up one day and find that I've aged."

I purse my lips through a smile, biting my tongue to keep from pointing out that she is a senior citizen, and aging is inevitable. "What are you saying, Karen?"

"Judy died. She didn't have one of us looking out for her. I think it's time I took a young lady under my wing and showed her the Live Forever way." Her chest swells at declaring this giant leap. Her assertive nod tells me she is certain this is the direction she wants her life to take. "Any nominations on who might benefit from a little extra Karen in her life?"

Marianne shrugs, but a name pops into my mind. "Heather is the hostess at the diner. She just lost her coworker. She might need a friend."

Karen points at me. "Done. I'll wash up and go kidnap her after that." She beams at us, truly looking younger and more radiant, even through the goo. "See? Each time I think it's going to be scary or too difficult to step out into something new, I'm surprised that the hardest part was making the decision itself."

These women inspire me. They open up my mind and make me see that the world is far grander than I ever imagined.

A decision firms in my chest. "Marianne, I'll be right back. I need to fix something."

"Okay, I'll be out here, practicing."

Karen disappears inside while Marianne poises her head at differing angles to see which might give her the best advantage when she goes to compete for the giant donut.

I love that sentences like that exist. Only in Sweetwater Falls.

My mind is racing as I dart into the kitchen, pulling out a notebook and pen to start sketching a design.

"What are you up to, Charlotte the Brave?" Agnes asks while Aunt Winnie washes her hands in the sink.

"I'm fixing an error. I played it too safe with my pumpkin spice cupcakes. They're supposed to be Halloween themed, but I chickened out and just colored the frosting orange. That's not scary. That's not what the people of Sweetwater Falls want." I sketch out a cupcake and jot a few notes on the side.

"You're going to put that on a cupcake?" Agnes inquires. Though, to her credit, her nose doesn't crinkle. "That is brave." She cups my shoulders. "Good for you!"

I am always grateful that they believe in my wild side.

If Karen can be brave and take in a girl like me who just needs a little push, then I can step outside of my comfort zone and fight harder for my passion.

As the cupcake sketch comes together, a devious smile sweeps across my face.

Sweetwater Falls wants a good scare?

Challenge accepted.

17

A LITTLE HELP FROM MY FRIENDS

*W*hen I show up for my shift, I am barely awake. To be fair, it isn't even dawn yet. No one should be out and about this early, especially if they were up late making peanut brittle with Logan and Marianne. Having an iron stomach built for taking in massive amounts of sweets is an underrated talent, I have learned.

When I open the front door of the diner, the sound of Bill's gruff raised voice hits my ears, smacking of rudeness. "I don't care if you feel like it, I need to be cooking today, or we won't have food to serve."

"Then just hire a new waitress already!" Heather yells back at him. "I didn't sign on to wait tables. I'm a hostess, and that's all."

"You're going to be out of job, young lady, if you keep up this attitude. You asked me for a raise last month, and I said no. Now I'm giving you the chance to earn full tips, instead of what you get when the waitstaff pools their tips, and you're acting like I've asked you to hunt around in the cracks searching for vermin. You want more money? This is how you get it."

I can practically picture Heather's eye roll, which I've seen her do on many occasions when she is asked to work a minute longer than her shift requires.

To be fair, I often rock that same eye roll, because Bill's requests are never-ending.

"I'm not waiting tables, Bill. End of story."

"Then go home for the day, Heather. End of story."

"I came in here to ask for time off. I have a trip I'm planning, and I need the time off to go. A week, Bill. I didn't come in here to talk about your inability to hire a new waitress."

"Do you have more vacation days, Heather?"

"No. You know I used them all up. But I really want to go. I need the time off. Seriously. It's only a week."

"You go on your trip, you can kiss your job goodbye. You can't use vacation days you don't have."

"Are you serious? You're not even going to consider it?"

"I'm not even going to discuss it."

I can practically picture Heather's fists clenched at her sides. "Fine!"

I do my best pretending act in order to appear as if I wasn't eavesdropping when Heather storms out of the kitchen. She punches her hands through the arms of her jacket, her eyes landing on me. "Enjoy Boss of the Year today, Charlotte. He's in a real mood. I'm supposed to go to a music festival with my friends out of state, and he won't give me the time off. Can you believe him?" Heather doesn't need me to respond. As she grabs up her purse, she pauses by the door near where I am standing. "Unbelievable. I finally have enough money to go, now that Judy's not skimming her tips when she was supposed to be pooling them, and I still can't go because of some archaic notion that people should only have two weeks each year of a break from this smelly place!"

I do my best to cast some understanding her way. "Judy was skimming tips? That's crummy."

Though I don't particularly love that we pool our tips at the end of each shift, it's standard business practice at a restaurant, so I never gave it more than an "aw, man!" sort of response.

"She was. And now Bill is treating me like I'm a child. Like I can't be in charge of my own time off."

Actually, he's treating you like an adult, holding you to the rules you agreed to when you started working here.

But I don't say that aloud. I can tell Heather isn't in the mood for logic.

Heather bristles as she hunts in her purse for her keys. "Oh, and you can tell Karen that I don't need to hang out with the Geriatric Dementia Club. I have enough friends, thank you very much. Unless she can find a way to get me out of work for the music festival, I'm not interested in spending quality time with Karen Newby." She curls her upper lip, as if the notion is preposterous.

"Excuse me?" Now it's my turn to throw a bit of attitude. Nobody talks about Karen like that when I'm around. "You'd better think again before insulting Karen for the horrible crime of being nice to you. Be mad at Bill all you want, but don't give Karen attitude because she wants to spend time with you."

Heather's upper lip curls. "Whatever. Enjoy double-duty."

What else is new?

I take my time removing my jacket and hanging it up, preparing myself for the morning rush that still hasn't died down in the time since Judy's passing. Apparently because there have been no other leads for people to gossip about, and I am still the one with the most information (being that I discovered her body), people have precious little else to do with their time than come into the diner, eat bad food and litter me with questions I don't want to discuss.

A six-hour shift turns into eight, with my feet ready to call it quits well before that. Bill has yet to hire another waitress, and the night shift isn't keen on working from opening until close. Bill has to help in the kitchen today, so the entire restaurant has one overwhelmed waitress.

When Bill tells me that the girl coming in for the evening shift to relieve me is running late, I nearly break down in tears. I didn't realize working two jobs would be this stressful, especially when cupcake orders are multiplying and waiting tables at the diner is becoming increasingly more arduous. A single shift is turning into a double, for which I am unprepared.

I had one break, which I had to use to drive out of the city to pick up the special ingredient for my Halloween cupcakes. I didn't get a chance to eat a thing. Then I got barked at by Bill because my break took five minutes too long.

And after this, I have to go home and start baking the hundreds of cupcakes for people to pick up tomorrow.

By the time I drag my feet into my car, I am an overly emotional wreck. I haven't cried, but I know it's coming. I should tell Bill I'm not coming back. I can't be the only waitress. While I know it takes time to hire someone new, the two-week notice expires in three days.

Three days.

The countdown used to fill me with excitement, but now all I feel is hopeless. Three more days of this isn't physically possible. I should have baked my cupcakes last night, but I used my free evening to make peanut brittle with Logan and Marianne. Though I got a few kisses out of the deal, I worry that when I check the tally of how many cupcakes I have to make tonight, I won't have enough time to fill all the orders *and* go to sleep.

By the time I get home, I am so stressed that I don't even smile when I see Marianne's sedan and Logan's navy pickup parked outside. My legs drag when I walk into the house, a brown package in my hand. I shed my jacket unartfully and groan as I pry my shoes off my feet.

"Charlotte? Is that you?" Marianne calls from the kitchen. I love that she's here, but I know I will make for terrible company tonight.

"Yeah. It's the version of me that exists after I've been asked about my dead coworker seven million times. I'm a bit fried." I move slowly toward the kitchen, unable to conjure up any semblance of pep. "How was your..." I stop in my tracks, my eyes widening and my mouth falling open. "What did you do?"

Marianne and Logan grin at me. "I've been given a promotion," Logan brags. "From dishwasher to Marianne's puppet. I'm learning how to make frosting. Brace yourself: I'm really good at it."

Hundreds and hundreds of cupcakes line the counters and the table. My brain takes in the image but refuses to process exactly what I am seeing. "I don't understand. What is... How did..."

Marianne beams proudly. "It's my day off. Since you used your free evening to teach me how to bake cheesecake and help me train for the donut event, I figured you could use some help tonight. I didn't realize Bill was going to keep you later than usual. He's really trying to get his full mileage out of your last two weeks, huh."

Logan's smile is a thing of beauty. "We decided to start baking, since we didn't know when you would be done. It's a good thing, too. Otherwise you would be working well into the night. We're nearly done with the baking part. All that's left to do is frost them."

I mean to thank them, but when I open my mouth, a weepy sound escapes. "You guys..."

Marianne blows me a kiss while Logan slides a chair out for me. "You must be exhausted. Winnie said you started before dawn. It's five o'clock, Miss Charlotte. Have you eaten dinner yet?"

I haven't had lunch, but I can't work out the words. Instead of speaking, I resort to shaking my head while tears of relief trickle down my cheeks.

Logan sets down the bowl of frosting and crouches between my knees, looking up into my stricken face. "Honey. What's wrong?" He takes the package from my hands that I picked up on my break today and sets it on the table so he can hold my hand.

I shake my head over and over, knowing that words are not my best option right now. I am so grateful for these two, showing up for me when I truly need it. My arms throw themselves around Logan's neck so I can cry on his shoulder. All the angst of my day spills out into the collar of his green polo shirt.

His arms go around me, lifting me to stand so he can hug me properly. "Hey, talk to me. Bad day at work?"

"Long day at work. Long, long day. Everyone wants to ask me about Judy, while all I want to do is my job. Actually, that's not true. I don't want to be there at all. I swear, once I'm just working the one job, I won't be so overwhelmed. I won't need this much help. I was dreading coming home and baking through the night. My feet are sore and I'm tired and... and..." I'm rambling incoherently, but I don't have the decorum left to care. "I was the only waitress all morning."

Logan presses his cheek to mine, holding me close so I don't have to find my footing in life just yet.

Marianne is flitting around the kitchen. She doesn't stop until Logan lowers me back into my chair. She slides a plate of food in front of me, her brows pushed together in concern. "Bill is overworking you. That's not right. Has he found a replacement for you yet? Your last day is coming up."

"No, and I don't think he's in any hurry to, either. I should have been like Heather this morning. He wanted her to wait tables, and she told him off. She stormed out instead of being a giant pushover, like me." My tears are starting to ebb, now that I've worked out the brunt of my overwhelm. "That you two started without me? I don't know what to say. I'm so grateful. I love baking cupcakes, and I hate that I don't love it tonight."

Marianne hugs my head to her side, running her hand across my back. "You're only one person, Charlotte. We've been taking up your time this week, and you haven't acted put out once. It's only fair we take something off your plate."

"I really, really needed the help tonight. Thank you."

Logan picks up the mixing bowl and displays its contents to me. "Not to distract you from your pain, but I might quit the force and make frosting full-time. Not the cupcakes part. Only frosting. I'm thinking of opening up a very specific type of restaurant."

I chuckle through my tears as I swipe them away. "Only frosting?"

Logan grins. "I mean, have you seen frosting this nice in your whole life?"

Marianne takes two trays out of the oven. "Heather really told Bill off? Not that I don't think he doesn't deserve it, but wow. I hope it didn't happen in front of the customers."

"No, it was before we opened. They were yelling at each other. Honestly, I'd be surprised if she shows up to work tomorrow at all."

Marianne grimaces. "Let's not go there in our minds until we have to. I'm sure Heather will cool down and Bill will get his act together in time for the morning shift tomorrow. Until then, Logan is living his best life, making more frosting than we could possibly use tonight. Good thing the stuff keeps. He's given you a head start on next week's cupcakes."

Logan postures proudly. "Because I'm a baker, now. The Frosting King." He jerks his head toward my goldfish. "Buttercream agrees."

I snigger at the two of them, wondering how I got so lucky.

Marianne points to my plate. "For now, you just eat. I don't remember how to make the pumpkin cream cheese frosting, so that gets to be you. Other than that, we've got this."

I do as I am told because frankly, I don't have the energy for much else. Marianne keeps taking breaks to refill my glass of water in between piping the fudge frosting atop the chocolate cupcakes. By the time I am ready to start in on the pumpkin cream cheese frosting, my head is clear, and I am ready to try something outside of my comfort zone.

I open the package that I purchased on my break today, knowing Winifred would probably not be thrilled to have this particular ingredient in her kitchen.

"Because you two took the heavy load off my shoulders, now I can have a bit of fun."

"Meaning?" Marianne inquires, pausing her piping to quirk her brow at me.

"Pumpkin Spice Cupcakes—a scream in every bite."

Marianne chuckles. "With a promise like that, you'd better deliver."

When I show them the contents of the mystery package, Marianne's face pulls in horror. Logan backs up, letting me know that I am on the right track.

Marianne's hand goes over her mouth. "You can't put that on a cupcake."

Logan blanches. "That is disgusting."

I examine the new ingredient. "Actually, it should only add a bit of crunch, not change the flavor of the cupcake. If Sweetwater Falls loves a good Halloween scare, I have to make sure I don't disappoint."

Marianne and Logan exchange looks of trepidation, but neither of them stops me when I open up the bag and ready myself to leap into the unknown.

Logan and Marianne give me and the bag a wide berth while I make the pumpkin cream cheese frosting and add my mystery ingredient as a topper. It's not until I am halfway through that Marianne calls my name. "Charlotte, your phone chimed. You've got a text."

"Oh, really? I didn't hear a thing."

"No kidding. You're really in the zone over there. Let me see..." She grimaces. "I thought you were doing normal piping over there! Are those... Did you make little brains with the frosting?"

I beam at her while Logan marvels at the design. "I sure did."

Marianne giggles at my enthusiasm. "And then that thing goes on top of the brain? Gross!"

"I'll take that as a compliment." I move to my phone and pull up my missed text. My shoulders fall. "Ugh. Bill wants me to come in and pick up a check. He's going out of town tomorrow, so I have to get it tonight." I frown at the screen. "Where is he going all of a sudden?" I close my eyes. "I don't want to go in right now, but I really don't want to have to wait until he gets back from wherever to get paid. The mystery ingredient wasn't cheap."

Logan bumps his hip to mine. "Hope you don't mind if that's the one cupcake of yours that I don't try. I'll just take your word on it being amazing."

Marianne waves me off. "Go get your check. We're all finished, Charlotte. All we have to do is clean up and box them all. I can get into the website to check the orders and box them up while Logan makes the kitchen sparkling clean."

Logan groans when he glances around at the wreckage. "Being the Frosting King has its downside. The dishwasher has fallen severely behind." He pecks my cheek when I make to argue that they have helped more than any person should ever be expected to. "We've got this. See you in a bit, Miss Charlotte."

I grab my coat and slide on my shoes, wondering how I got to be so lucky. I think the same thing on my drive to the diner and am miraculously still smiling when I enter my workplace well after operational hours. The front of the house lights are off, but the kitchen is illuminated.

"Bill?" I call through the diner as I make my way toward the kitchen. "Bill, I'm here. Do you have my..."

But my words stop short when my eyes fall on my boss sprawled out on the floor. His eyes are open, and he is gagging on a foam that's burbling out of his mouth.

"Bill! Oh, Bill! No!" I dash to his side, unsure what to do, other than call for an ambulance in hopes that they will know how to help in this dire situation. I drop to my knees while he chokes on something that he clearly should never have ingested.

When he vomits on the greasy floor, I realize that it is the same pink bubbly stuff I saw when I found Judy in her car.

Whoever came after Judy is trying to take down Bill, too.

18

BARELY BREATHING BILL

anic grips me around the throat as I hold onto Bill's hand. "Can you tell me who did this?" I ask him, though I know any breath he still has left should be conserved. The kitchen is in its usual state of a post-shift attempt at cleanliness. I cast around for clues, wondering what could have done this to him.

Once again, I am struck by the fact that I know next to nothing about the person I work with, aside from his terrible taste in soup. Does he have family I should be calling? Does he have someone he would rather be holding hands with if these are, in fact, his last moments?

I do my best to murmur soothing things to him while his eyes bug. "Bill, I'm right here. I won't leave you alone. The paramedics are on their way. Hold on, Bill! Help is coming." Though I'm not sure if my words hold any weight, I repeat them over and over while the seconds tick by. The paramedics keep me on the phone, but they give me no way to help him. I would do whatever they ask, but only a professional can save Bill now.

Still holding tight to his hand, I cast around to see if I can spot the murder weapon. It has to be a poison of some sort. "Bill, what did you eat or drink? I think you were poisoned!"

But it's clear Bill cannot hear me right now. I hold tight to his hand while I scan the kitchen, hoping to find whatever it is that brought Bill to his knees.

The dishes are washed.

There is a glass of water on the counter, but it looks full.

The cup of soup resting on the counter beside the glass of water calls to me.

It would be the perfect crime, putting poison in Bill's soup. He eats the stuff for lunch and dinner, so of course poisoning the soup would be an easy way to take out Bill. And the taste is so terrible and rubbery, it would most likely hide the tang of the foreign element.

I close my eyes, praying aloud for the paramedics to come quick. I can't see inside the bowl without letting go of Bill's hand, but I can imagine its empty contents well enough. The man inhales the broccoli and cheese slop, never tiring of the same burnt flavor and poor excuse for a scant serving of vegetables.

I am sweating, terrified that Bill might die before help gets here. The emergency line operator is trying to talk me down, but she isn't giving me a way to save Bill's life. "Help me!" I shout through fresh tears. "I don't know what to do!"

Almost as soon as I call out the plea, I hear the front doors open.

"Back here in the kitchen!" I call, relieved when I hear the heavy tread of at least two bodies coming to rescue my boss.

I have never been more grateful to see anyone in my life. The man and woman in paramedic jackets rush in and take over. I am slid out of the way while they administer something liquid, black and thick to Bill. I want to look away, but I am transfixed when they are miraculously able to get it down his throat.

It is an eternity before Bill is breathing, but his shallow gasps bring relief and life to my soul. I feel as if my own chest has been constricted and can at last move on its own. My hand cups my sobs while my phone trembles in my grip. Before the next minute passes, I know I need to call Logan. Not just the police, but Logan himself. I am sure the paramedics alerted the police already anyway, but this is something I should tell him directly. Logan is off duty right now, so he wouldn't get the call to come in and investigate what I am certain is an attempt at murder.

My phone connects with Logan's. I don't bother putting my words in any cohesive order when he answers. "Everything okay, Miss Charlotte? You've been gone a while."

"It's too coincidental to be an accident," I blurt out. Then I grimace. I knew that once I started speaking, it would come out all jumbled. "Judy and now him. The pink vomit is bubbly." I cringe, unsure when the last time was that I described vomit in such vivid detail. I don't want to compare types of barf, but I know that if I am going to draw a line from one point to another, I have to be perfectly factual. "He couldn't breathe!"

The paramedics move Bill onto a gurney and wheel him out of the kitchen while Logan forsakes his Frosting King hat and dons his officer of the law demeanor. "Whoa, one thing at a time. Who couldn't breathe? Are you at the diner?"

"He's breathing now. Or, I think I saw him breathe. But is it only temporary before his breathing stops for good? Did they fix it, or is it a band-aid that postpones the inevitable for a little while?" Panic grips me afresh. "I should have gone with them! What if he dies and no one is there to hold his hand? I have to go!"

Logan's voice comes back to me with a firmness that straightens my spine and stills my exit. "Charlotte, where are you? I'm on my way to the diner. Is that where you are?"

I nod, but then realize he can't see me. "The diner, yes. But should I go to the hospital? What should I do?"

Logan's command is solid. "Stay right where you are. If the man can't breathe and he's being taken to the hospital, that is the best place for him." Logan pauses, and I hear the roar of his pickup. "Now first things first: are you okay? Are you safe?"

I nod, but again realize after the fact that he cannot see me. "Yes. I'm in the diner. I came in and found Bill on the floor in the kitchen. He had the same kind of puke that Judy had when I found her."

Logan's sadness is a true mark that he hasn't lost his humanity to the job, no matter how long he's been at it. "Oh, that's terrible. Poor Bill."

"He could barely breathe when I came in. I called for an ambulance, but I didn't know how to help him! It's poison, right? He was poisoned! Just like Judy."

"I'm on my way, honey."

Even though I am flustered and frightened, Logan's gentle way serves to settle parts of me that might have remained mixed up for days without his sweetness. "Hurry," I beg in a whisper. "I'm not touching anything, but I'm pretty sure it was the soup."

"What was the soup? What do you mean? Is that how Bill was poisoned?"

I rub my forehead. "I don't know! I don't know. I'm scared, Logan. Or I'm sad. I don't know. How could someone do such a thing? Twice!"

Logan's even cadence serves to center the fearful parts of me. "Stay right where you are. Don't touch a thing. We're nearly there."

"We?"

"Marianne and Winifred are following behind me. You didn't think I would show up without your girls, do you? And I'm sure Winifred called Karen and Agnes. Hold tight, Miss Charlotte. We're on our way."

I love how well he knows me, even though we have only

been together a short time. He knows that Marianne and I understand each other, and that the Live Forever Club stands with their girls, no matter how gruesome the crime scene.

I hold onto the counter once I end the call with Logan. Steadying my breath is hard but becomes impossible when my gaze falls to the cup of soup on the stainless-steel counter. The spoon is plunged into the gelatinous slop, but to my surprise, it doesn't look like more than a bite or two has been eaten. Usually Bill inhales his soup, I presume without bothering to taste how terrible it is first.

Thank goodness he only took a bite or two. I cannot imagine the state in which I would have found him if he had consumed the entire thing.

Actually, I have quite the vivid imagination, and can picture Bill in the exact state I found him, minus the gasping breaths.

I cast around for any other clue that might inform my verdict. I need all the proof I can get to confirm that this was the weapon used with the intent of taking Bill down.

The stainless-steel countertop is cleared. The floor isn't swept, but that's nothing new. Crumbs litter the floor near the prep station. My shoes have the usual sticky feel they get whenever I walk into the kitchen.

My gaze falls on a scrap of paper near where I found Bill on the floor. I kneel down to pick it up, unfolding the crinkled corner so I can make out the bubbly letters scribbled across the paper.

BILL,

YOU SHOULD HAVE KNOWN NOT TO CROSS ME.

. . .

-Charlotte

My intake of breath is the only sound filling my ears, so much that when Logan, Marianne and Winifred race inside, their presence takes me by surprise.

Logan gets out his phone and calls his father while Marianne sidesteps the vomit and gathers me in her arms. Winifred's hand rubs my back, but not even a steady stream of kindness from these two can quell the storm that rages inside of me.

I have no words, even as I hand the note to Logan. He asks me where I found it, but all I can do is mouth helplessly that I didn't write it.

I didn't kill Bill, but somebody out there wants the world to think that I did.

19

KITCHEN QUESTIONING

*I*t is humiliating to be questioned by the guy I am dating's father. Even more so with Logan chiming in every now and then to correct his dad's tone. The sheriff has a brusque demeanor to him, which I can appreciate, but it does nothing to put me at ease. I was under the impression from television crime dramas that there would be a good cop and bad cop sort of scenario in these types of situations, but so far, all I have managed to come across is one very grumpy sheriff.

"You decided to do some light cleaning while you were smack in the middle of a crime scene? Why did you pick up this paper from the floor?" The sheriff's thick salt and pepper brows knit together.

I shrug, my reason sounding stupid when it comes out of my mouth. "I was looking for clues."

His chin dimple deepens in time with his displeasure, his square jaw twitching. "Do you fancy yourself a detective?"

I frown at him, doing my best not to display attitude or anything that might look like culpability. "No, I fancy myself a baker."

"And a waitress, right? I mean, that was your boss who was wheeled out of here."

"Yes, sure. I'm a waitress, too. I put in my two weeks though." As soon as I say this, I know it was the wrong thing to tell him.

The sheriff scribbles something in his notepad. "How did Bill treat his staff?"

I rub my forehead, wishing this whole thing would go away. "Like a boss? I don't know. Am I in trouble?"

"It looks that way, doesn't it."

Logan frowns at his father while his partner, Wayne, bags evidence in the background. "She has an alibi, Dad. *I* am her alibi if you recall. Stop giving Charlotte a hard time. You know she didn't do it. She's the one who called the ambulance and reported it to the police."

The sheriff taps his pen on the edge of his notepad. "Actually, she reported it to her boyfriend. She *should* have called the police."

My heart sinks at how guilty that sounds.

Logan tilts his head at his father. "And she just so happened to leave a signed confession in the kitchen? She's obviously being framed, Dad."

Winifred holds my hand under the table. She hasn't left my side this entire time.

The sheriff leans back in his seat. "I know that, Son."

My racing heartrate begins to slow. "You do?"

The sheriff shoots me a wry look as if to ask if I have gone crazy. "Whoever did this clearly thought Bill would have been dead by the time you got here. You showed me the text that lured you to the diner afterhours. I asked you if you fancy yourself a detective because this isn't the first crime scene we've met at, young lady. I don't want you in this situation again."

"Yes, sir." I don't want to be in this situation again, either.

"Next time you find a body on the floor, call the professionals and then don't touch anything. Not the scrap of paper on the floor. Nothing. Now that thing's got your fingerprints on it."

My expression falls. "Oh my goodness. I didn't even think of that. I'm so sorry!"

"I know, I know. And I asked you how Bill treated his staff because there is no sign that whoever came in here broke in. Either the person had a key, or Bill recognized them and let them inside. So, tell me truthfully, how is it working here?"

I don't want to say anything bad about a man who is currently fighting for his life. "It's not horrible. Paychecks are on time."

"Logan's mentioned that you have been working extra hours, and that you're understaffed."

"Sure, but that's hardly Bill's fault. Judy was our other morning shift waitress, and she isn't with us any longer."

"I see." The sheriff scribbles in his notepad.

I clear my throat, searching through my brain to see what tidbits might be useful. "Whoever did this knows Bill. That's true. But it's more than that Bill recognized the person and let them in. They really know him. Know his habits and preferences. Bill has a cup of that awful soup for lunch and dinner every single day. If I was going to poison him, which I didn't," I pause, making sure the sheriff heard that last part, "that's how I would do it. You might want to have Wayne dump out the whole vat of soup."

The sheriff nods, writing in his notepad. "That's very helpful. I wouldn't worry about coming in for your shift tomorrow. This whole place is a crime scene, so you've got yourself the next day or two off. If I have any further questions, I'll stop on by."

Winifred frowns at him from her spot by my side. "See that you bring a sunnier disposition when you do. This mug of yours does nothing to put the distressed at ease. Honestly, Louis. You sounded like you were interrogating my niece. You need to work on your bedside manner."

Sheriff Flowers doesn't look all too happy to be on the business end of Winifred's scolding. He stands, nodding to my great-aunt. "See that you take this one straight home and get her some tea. When I hear anything about Bill's condition, I'll let you know."

Marianne helps me up, taking hold of my elbow to steer me toward the exit. "Everything is going to be okay," she promises me, though how she can make that assertion, I am not entirely sure. "You're not being arrested. Bill is alive, as far as we know. The sheriff is right; let's get you home."

I'm scared. Even when we cross the threshold into the house, my legs are still rubbery. For the second time today, Marianne helps me to sit in a chair at the kitchen table. For the second time today, I marvel at how much work was done while I was away.

"Did you box up all the cupcakes while I was gone?"

Marianne turns on the kettle. "I sure did. And Logan finished the dishes. The sheriff was right; you need some hot tea and sleep. I'll work on the tea."

Winifred holds up her finger. "I'll work on the sleep part. I'll run a hot bath with some of my lavender bath salts for you, dear."

"You guys don't have to do all that. I'm okay. Bill is the one who is having a horrible night."

Winifred shakes her head. "Poor Bill. I can't stand the thought of a repeat killer living among us. Whoever did that to Bill has to be the same person who killed Judy. Same method, it looks like."

Marianne takes down the box of chamomile from the cupboard. "Who would Judy and Bill have both upset? It has to be a customer at the diner. That's their only connection."

Winifred's lips purse. "Maybe Judy served bad food, so they retaliated, but then they realized Bill is the person who cooks most of the food, so they went for him instead? Have you girls heard of anyone getting food poisoning lately?"

Marianne shakes her head. "That would be a question for Delia. She knows more about what goes on in Sweetwater Falls than I do."

Winifred moves slowly upstairs. I sit in silence while Marianne makes tea and Winifred runs the bath for me.

"I don't know what people do without family like you both. This whole day is so awful. And you and Logan finished the orders without me? I don't deserve you."

Marianne sits down and covers my hand with hers. "Yes, you do. And I know that you would do the exact same thing if our roles were reversed. Hang in there, Charlotte. We will find out who did this. Until then, we are locking the doors and only eating food we have prepared. Got it?"

I hate that precautions like this are necessary. "Do you really think the murderer is targeting people who work at the diner?"

"I really think it's a possibility, so we're not taking any chances. I'm spending the night, okay?"

"You don't have to do that. I know you must be exhausted."

Marianne opens her mouth to quell my protest, but she is interrupted by the doorbell. She stands, coming back half a minute later with Agnes and Karen, who are both in their pajamas. Karen is wearing a sexy silk pant and camisole set, and Agnes is wearing a red flannel nightdress down to her ankles that has long sleeves and a frilly lace neckline.

Agnes tugs me out of my chair and wraps me in a hug I desperately need. "Oh, dear. This is nothing a pajama party won't fix. I was working on a papier-mâché craft, which can wait."

"What?"

"Winifred called us, so we came right over. Tonight is all about Cary Grant, popcorn and cookie dough."

Karen sets a giant lidded bowl on the table. "I brought the popcorn."

"And I keep cookie dough in my freezer for just such an occasion."

I chuckle, surprised anything is funny tonight. "You keep cookie dough at the ready for when someone's boss is nearly murdered?"

Agnes kisses my cheek. "Cookie dough is for the unsolvable headaches. Tonight, we drown our sorrows the proper way: with girlfriends and Cary Grant. He's the only man with a perpetual invite."

I hug Agnes tighter than I mean to, and for a second, I'm not sure I can let go. Everything feels jumbled and upside-down. I need her hug to keep the world from crashing around me.

"It's alright, dear. It's alright."

Though her promises couldn't feel farther from the truth, I let Agnes' sweet demeanor soothe my angst as much as she is able. Though I shouldn't be surprised that I am not alone during a truly terrible evening, my heart swells all the same.

I love these women, and am grateful that this awful night isn't also a lonely one.

20

MOTIVATIONS FOR MURDER

*I*t's been a long time since I slept in. Not having to work at the diner Friday morning is the only upside to this whole horrible thing. Marianne and I slept in the living room with Marianne on the couch and me in a sleeping bag on the floor so that Agnes and Karen could share my bed upstairs. After the Live Forever Club turned in for the night, Marianne and I stayed up running over the evidence and basically obsessing until not even the shred of a path we had before made a lick of sense.

There may have been too much cookie dough involved.

I take my time getting ready in the morning, and don't properly greet everyone until I am dressed and I have a cup of tea in my hand. Even then I mostly communicate in grunts and half sentences while the ladies bustle around the kitchen.

Well, Agnes and Winifred bustle about the kitchen while Karen and I drink tea together and Marianne occupies the shower.

"I've been thinking about things," Karen muses quietly while Agnes whisks eggs, ham, onions and green peppers in a bowl.

"What kinds of things?"

"Usually only the tawdry, but today I've been putting my mind to less amusing use." She takes a long sip, pursing her lips while she stares into her teacup. "The person who has the most to gain from Judy dying also has something to gain from Bill biting it. Either Bill saw something he shouldn't have and he was being silenced, or whoever killed Judy developed a taste for solving their problems with poison."

My shoulders slump. "I hate everything about this."

Karen is unperturbed that I am ill equipped for macabre conversations. "I don't think Bill saw something damning. I think it's the latter theory: that whoever did this is more than capable of killing their conscience entirely so they can do it again and again—however many times it suits their interests."

I run my finger along the edge of my teacup. "So far I haven't come across anything Judy did to anyone that might spark that sort of extreme reaction. The two people she borrowed money from seemed unmotivated to get it back."

Karen sets down her teacup. "Did you tear up at the movie last night?"

I turn my head, confused at her abrupt change in topic. "I mean, sure, but it's Cary Grant. I'm not sure anyone can get through a Cary Grant movie without feeling a little bit of something."

"And when you came down here, did you greet your goldfish by name?"

I narrow my eyes at Karen. "I'm not sure what you're getting at, but yes. Buttercream is a good person." I catch my odd phrasing and chuckle.

Karen points a crooked finger at me. "You do those things because you're a sweet girl. You're judging possible motivations for murder under your Girl Scout filter of sweetness. You would never consider killing for something you deem unimportant, but that's not the mind of a murderer. You need to adjust your filter."

My mouth pulls to the side. "I'm not sure how to do that."

Karen runs her finger around the rim of her teacup. "Lower the bar. Instead of unpaid debts, think of people Judy may have sneezed on."

My nose crinkles. "You can't be serious."

Karen's gaze makes it seem like her mind is very far away, like she is thinking of things that aren't in this room or even in this timeframe. I know very little about her life before I showed up in Sweetwater Falls. I wonder what sort of stories she has been part of, and how they inform the magnificent woman she is today.

When she finally replies, her voice is grave. "People convince themselves of all sorts of things to throw themselves into a victim's light. They will tell themselves anything to prove that the ends justify the means." She blinks and then turns to me, bringing herself back to the present. "Now tell me anyone Judy has offended, no matter how small the matter."

I drag in a deep breath, wondering if my stabs in the dark might eventually allow light to shine on the evidence, framing it in a whole new way. Whoever did this had either legitimate problems or minor aggravations with Bill and Judy.

Agnes pours the egg mixture into a skillet, shaking it a few times to make sure the eggs don't stick irreparably to the pan.

Winifred's back is to me while she chops the heads off strawberries, ensuring we have a luxurious breakfast after our night of bonding.

My mind makes a few ungraceful stops and starts as I switch to Karen's way of thinking. I dig through my brain for any affront that Judy may have caused.

The list of irritations Bill may be responsible for is too long to start.

"I mean, if we're going by anyone who might be miffed with a waitress, that's not a list with an end to it. People blame us for their food tasting bad. They blame us for the bill being what it is. They blame us for the kitchen being backed up. Any of those things could have gotten Judy killed if we're dropping the bar that low."

Karen nods, taking her time before dismissing the notion altogether. "Anyone in particular who mentioned an irritation with Judy?"

I shrug, but then a face pops into my mind. I try to push it away because to point the finger at someone for something so trivial seems unfair. I lower my voice, my hands warming around my cup. "If I say someone, it's not me accusing them of murder, right? We're just brainstorming."

Marianne trots into the room, her short hair still damp. "No bad ideas in brainstorming!" she sings.

Man, we needed that slumber party last night. Even though the dark cloud of murder still hangs over us, being together so none of us has to puzzle through it all alone relaxes me in ways I know I could not achieve on my own.

I chew on my lower lip. "Heather mentioned that Judy was skimming tips. We're supposed to pool our tips at the end of our shift, so the hostess gets a bump in her pay, too. I don't know if it's true or not, but Heather said Judy wasn't putting her full tips into the pot. I guess Judy kept some back for herself."

Karen nods once. "If I was in the mood for murder, that might be reason enough. Did Heather have issues with Bill?"

"I mean, Bill isn't exactly a snuggly bunny." Another nagging idea tugs at my brain. "I overheard them arguing earlier this week. She didn't have any vacation days left and she wanted a week off to go to some music festival out of state. He said no. It got pretty heated." I rub

my forehead. "But that can't be motive for murder."

Agnes shakes the pan again, keeping her eyes on the eggs. "I ate an entire carton of ice cream in one sitting once. It was the day I buried my husband of thirty years."

The room quiets to show respect to the obvious pain in poor Agnes' heart.

She flips the eggs deftly without making a mess of the omelet, as only one who has tackled the task hundreds of times can do with such confidence. "I had never done it before, but after that, it got easier. I don't do that anymore, but at the time, after I did it once, it wasn't so shocking when I did it again. And again."

Winifred sets down her knife and kisses Agnes on the temple. "Bernard was a good man."

Agnes dons a weathered smile that bespeaks a gentleness that has not soured with time. "Yes, he was. My point is that when you do something crazy the first time, it can be not so shocking to do it again—especially if there are no consequences. Whoever murdered Judy didn't get caught. So when Bill vexed them, it wasn't such a fight with their conscience to go that same route."

The logic is tragic but makes sense. "That breaks my optimism a little," I admit.

Karen motions to the goldfish bowl on the windowsill. "Marianne, be a love and fetch Buttercream. I think Charlotte might need the extra boost."

Marianne complies, taking care with Buttercream as she sets the precious little fish in its bowl before me on the table. I love watching the cutie swim about. I let myself enjoy the distraction for a minute, but then return to the unsolvable problem. "Then the issue becomes proving who it could be. If it is Heather, we need proof."

Karen nods. "Now, you're thinking. Any chance you could become a mild irritation to her?"

Winifred turns with disapproval firm on her face. "I don't like the idea of dangling my niece in front of a murderer as bait."

Karen holds up her hands. "Fair point. Just brainstorming. I'll give it some more thought."

When Logan's call interrupts our morning, I nearly jump on the phone. "Logan, did you hear anything about Bill? Is he okay?"

Logan's voice is scratchy, which makes me think he's been up all night long. "Bill is alive, yes. They're looking to see how much damage has been done to his throat that might be long-term, but for now, he's alright. Awake and alert, as much as he is able to be, after the long night he's had."

My heart races as I cut to the heart of it. "Does he know who poisoned him?"

Logan's pause does nothing to quell my spiking nerves. "He knows it wasn't you, so there's that. Your name is cleared."

"I guess that's progress." I should be more joyful that Bill could confirm I am not on the list of people possibly responsible for his intended murder.

"He said he hadn't seen you since you got off your last shift, so he knows you didn't poison him. They were serving that soup all evening after you clocked out, so you couldn't have poisoned the pot he ate from. And the poisoning happened after the diner closed for the night, because none of the customers fell ill or died from consuming the soup."

"So it was someone who came in afterhours."

Logan's voice is grave. "That narrows it down to staff who closed last night, which was not you."

I tick off a list of people who were on the schedule last night. Two waitresses and a line cook.

"Heather wasn't on the schedule?"

"No, there isn't a hostess in the evening during the week—only on weekends."

Logan pauses. "So she had no reason to be there after close."

"I mean, not unless someone took Bill's phone and texted her from it, like they did me to lure me there to take the blame for the murder."

"Bill saw Heather after close. I assumed she was on the schedule." I can picture perfectly Logan's serious face while he comes to the same conclusion I am racing toward. "I can request access to Heather's phone. If there is no text from Bill's number asking her to come in, then there is no reason she should have been there. When I spoke to Bill this morning, he said she was asking him for time off again while he was having his dinner after close, but he said no. She left, and that was that."

"Heather was the last person to see Bill before he was poisoned. Am I hearing that right?"

"That's correct." Logan's voice takes on an edge of compassion. "You're at home, right? Doors are locked?"

"Yes. I'm with the girls. We had a sleepover last night, the five of us."

A sliver of amusement creeps into his tone. "That's good. Can you do me a favor and stay inside today? I need to know that you're safe. If it is Heather, she has now killed or tried to kill two people at your workplace. I'm being overly cautious because I care about you, but if you could keep me from worrying myself sick by staying inside (and with someone) until this is settled and we rule Heather out as a suspect, I would greatly appreciate it."

Karen raises her hand from her seat beside mine, silently volunteering to stay with me until Heather is apprehended.

I reach over and hold Karen's hand. "That's the plan. I have the day off, so I'll be at home all day."

"Good. Tell Buttercream I picked up new food for her. I poked around online and found some stuff that can give her a better slime coat."

I blanch at his phrasing, but the sentiment rings like a bell through my heart. "That's so nice of you. Thank you."

"Tell her I miss her?"

My neck shrinks and a blush creeps onto my cheeks because I know he's talking about me, too. "I can do that."

"Tell her I want her to stay safe, alright? I'll come and read to her tomorrow if I get some time away from the precinct."

I take a chance and go for unvarnished honestly. "I really like you, Logan."

Logan goes silent. I can tell how unused to verbal affection he is from me. "I really like you, too, Miss Charlotte."

When we end the call, Winifred is grinning from ear to ear. Agnes grabs her up in a dance and starts waltzing around the kitchen while the two of them repeat the cutesy parts of our conversation. "I really like you, Agnes!" Winifred coos.

"I really like you, too, Winifred!"

Karen's smile tells me she is enjoying the merriment, but there is a shrewd focus to her gaze. Her mind is working over-time, factoring in the evidence that looks like it might be leading straight toward Heather.

21

SURPRISE COFFEE

I never get to field the cupcake pickups. I'm always at the diner, so Winifred manages the people who filter in and out of the house all morning on Fridays to pick up their cupcake orders. I love that today I get to greet my customers.

My customers. I love the sound of that. I have a real business with real customers, all based on doing the one thing I love. If life can get better, I am not sure how. The smell of frosting still lingers in the air. Marianne took one of the extra cupcakes to work, claiming she didn't want to go a day without a dessert. There are always a couple of random cupcakes leftover, which the girls and I munch on after the orders are filled.

Agnes and Winifred are working in the garden while Karen tests her patience teaching me how to play bridge. "You're supposed to hold your cards to your chest," Karen instructs me.

I don't understand the point of that, since she cannot see my cards from where I sit. But I suppose learning the mannerisms that make a Bridge player seem legit is worth trying. Buttercream swims in her bowl beside me at the kitchen table, greeting me with her fluttery tail each time I sit back down from answering the doorbell and handing out a person's order.

I check on my cactus, admiring how healthy it looks. I silently congratulate myself that I have not killed this plant that Logan and I bought together not too long ago.

The cupcakes are more than halfway handed out, but I am no nearer to understanding the loopholes in this stinking card game. I plan on asking Marianne if this is something we truly need to learn, and if so, can she please teach me an easier, abbreviated version.

When the doorbell rings again, I set my cards down and move toward the door, my smile freezing awkwardly on my face when none other than Heather stands on my porch. Her teenaged complexion greets me with a pop of her pink gum. Her eyes focus on me in a way that seems calculating. Being that she barely makes eye contact whenever I speak to her at work, this hits me as odd. "Can I help you?"

Heather holds my gaze, clutching two to-go cups of coffee. "Shame about Bill," she muses.

It's a strangely direct way to be greeted, but I do my best to roll with it. "It really is. But hey, you get to go to your music festival, right?"

Heather pops her gum. "Funny thing. The police don't want me to leave town. Seems they think I had something to do with it." She looks me up and down. "Though, since you're hanging out here, maybe they're telling all the employees the same thing. I heard you found Bill's body."

I stiffen, sweat dampening my nape. "Who told you that?"

Heather's mouth firms. "Word gets around. Here. I thought you could use a pick-me-up, being that you had a rough night. Shame finding Bill like that." Heather hands me one of the cups in her hand and pushes past me into the house, as if I have invited her inside. "Did Bill have anything on him? Any reason the police suspect us?"

I want to protest that the police don't suspect me of anything (anymore), but I keep that tidbit to myself.

"Nothing of note. I don't really want to talk about it. You went out and got me coffee? That was nice of you."

"I can be warm on occasion. Rare occasion," she quips with a smirk. "The sooner we get this solved, the sooner I can go to my music festival. I thought we could have some coffee and try to figure out who poisoned Bill together. I'm sure you're not enjoying house arrest any more than I am."

I point to her obvious presence in my home. "It doesn't look like you're on house arrest."

Heather rolls her eyes. "You know what I mean." She points to the cup in my hand. "Try to keep up, new girl. Caffeine helps with that."

I clutch the steaming cup as dread rises in my throat.

If Heather killed Judy and then tried to murder Bill, then she is the one who tried to frame me. Both of those seemed to have happened via poisoning.

Suddenly the cup of coffee doesn't have the offering of friendship to it, but the sting of something far more deadly. My instinctive urge is to dump it out in the sink, but I know that what I am holding might actually be a cup filled with evidence.

When Heather moves into the kitchen, she stops short. "Oh. Hi, Karen. I didn't realize you would be here this early in the morning."

"Yes, well, I decided to stay with my girl to help pass out cupcakes today." Karen's smile widens, revealing her broad dentures that don't quite fit her slender face. "Now I have two lovely girls to spend my morning with. My, what a lucky woman I am."

Karen pulls out a seat for Heather, holding her gaze so there is no mistaking that Heather will be sitting at the table with us. As Heather complies, Karen winks at me over her shoulder, and then narrows her gaze at the cup of coffee in my hand, letting me know that she is on the same thought train that I am.

We are in silent agreement that neither of us is going to drink that coffee.

Karen takes a seat at the table and motions for me to sit, as well. She places her hand atop Heather's with all the pandering sweetness in the world packed into her saccharine tone. "You poor dear. What a horrible mess this all is. I've known Bill since he was a boy, you know."

Heather snorts. "I can't imagine him little. He's so old."

I purse my lips to keep something tart from spewing out at her, but Karen is well-versed in hospitality, more so than I am. She conjures up a delighted cackle. "Oh, yes. When Bill was younger, he used to bag groceries. Then he helped ladies like me carry our groceries to our cars for a nickel a bag."

Heather offers a simpering smile, batting her lashes. "What a saint."

"Far from it, but still, it's horrid to think that anyone would try to hurt someone in our little haven. I can't imagine the broken soul who would attempt such a thing. Whoever it is must be getting anxious, knowing how close they are to being caught."

Heather's brow quirks. "How's that? They didn't find anything at the crime scene, I thought." She glances toward me, and I can tell she is wondering why the letter framing me wasn't mentioned.

My mouth is dry and my hands are clammy. I don't know how Karen is so calm and charismatic. I can barely work out a sentence, for fear of pointing my finger at Heather and screaming that she should be ashamed of herself for murdering Judy and poisoning Bill.

I'm guessing that's not how the professionals do it.

I need to call Logan, but that would be a dead giveaway that we are onto her. If Heather has tried her hand at murdering twice, I would imagine it's not all that difficult for her to give it another go. It's not me I am most worried about if a physical altercation comes. Karen has moxie for days, but she can't weigh more than a hundred pounds, if that.

Karen's eyes seem to darken. "The guilty party will be found soon enough. Don't you pretty little dears lose sleep over that. Murder takes a toll on even the most polluted of souls. They become a shadow of a person." She locks her eyes onto Heather's. "Shadows are easy enough to spot in broad daylight."

I marvel at Karen's poetry even as she stands, rummaging in the fridge as if she uttered nothing profound at all. She pulls out my container of extra fudge frosting with a maternal smile. Logan did indeed make way more than enough.

Karen takes my coffee cup from my hand and snatches Heather's, too. "Oh, you have to try coffee the way my Charlotte takes it. Simply delightful. Too sweet for my liking, but I know you'll love it, Heather."

I mean, sure, there's extra frosting in the fridge—there always is—but it's not the abrupt switch in topics I was counting on.

Heather leans forward. "I don't need..."

But it's too late for her protest. Karen has already popped the lids off of both and turned her back to us, setting them on the counter, one behind the other, so there is no way of telling whose is whose.

My spine lengthens as amazement floods my features.

Brilliant woman.

A scoop of frosting is plopped into both cups, and then Karen frowns at my goldfish. "Oh, my. Charlotte, Buttercream isn't looking so good. Can you request some of that special food be brought over? I know someone mentioned it to you. Tell them yes, bring over the special food, and hurry." Karen rinses both lids off in the sink and then pops them back into place. "Goldfish are delicate creatures."

My heart is racing as I absorb the clear message in Karen's command. "I can do that." I go to my purse and pull out my phone, my fingers quaking as I type an emergency text to Logan. We have the steaming hot evidence. All we need is an officer to make the arrest.

Now.

Heather looks every bit as put out as I would expect when a killer's attempt at a murder is foiled by a simple coffee cup mix-up. When Karen sets both cups in the center of the table, she appears relaxed and at ease with her clever coup. Now there is no way to tell which cup is safe for Heather to drink, and which has the poison inside of it.

Karen smiles at Heather. "Funny thing. There was a piece of evidence at the crime scene. Odd that the police didn't share that information with you."

Heather perks up. "There was?"

"Indeed. Charlotte found a note next to Bill while he was choking on his own sick. It said, *'You should have known not to cross me.'* Then it had your name signed at the bottom, dear." Karen shakes her head, looking genuinely perplexed. "Why wouldn't they have told you that someone was trying to frame you, Heather?"

I balk at Karen, wondering what angle it is that she's playing. That's what the note said, but it was signed with my name, not Heather's.

Heather opens her mouth, indignant. "That's not what it..." She stops short, catching herself too late.

In that moment, there is no shred of doubt that I am in the presence of Judy's killer and Bill's attacker.

Heather straightens in her seat, pushing her hair back over

her ears. "Is that so? Well, it makes sense why they don't want me to leave town, then. I'm being framed."

Karen leans in, patting Heather's hand. "Now don't you think it would be better for you if you just confessed, dear?"

Heather's denial flares in her face, but then crests to a firm malice that her secret has been found out.

I guess we aren't going to wait for the police to get here before our coffee time comes to blows.

22

HEATHER UNHINGED

*H*eather dives for the coffees at the same time I do. One tips over, but she manages to grab the other, popping the top off with a snarl as Karen gets up from her seat. She turns to Karen, but I dart in front of my friend as the coffee flies through the air. I scream when the steaming liquid splashes across my face, chest and arm, but it was worth it if Karen can escape unscathed.

"Run, Karen!" I order my friend. I have precious little prowess with physical conflict, but I figure running at Heather is my best move. I charge at her but realize quickly that her need to get out of going to jail is a greater motivator than my need to see her arrested. Heather is far stronger than I realized, and I quickly find myself being shoved up against the stove.

Heather's eyes possess a mad gleam about them, now that all pretense is gone. "You don't understand! Judy was stealing from me! Skimming tips is theft! I stole her journal to see how she liked being robbed, but she never came forward to make things right."

"Then Judy was stealing from me, too, since we share our tips." I work out while Heather and I grapple with each other to fend off the other's attack. "You don't see me murdering anybody."

When I finally manage to get Heather's hands off me, I make the mistake of allowing myself a breath of relief instead of lunging to pummel her.

Heather winds up and clocks me across the face, frightening me with how much power she has packed in her punch. The sound of my own scream scares me as it announces to the house how painful that was.

Heather slams me back against the counter again while my head spins. "Did your boyfriend get you out of looking guilty? Did Logan tear up the note for you?" Heather sneers as she coils her hands around my throat.

I claw at her wrists, trying to work my thumb beneath her grip on me so I can choke in a breath or two.

This isn't how I thought I would die. I pictured growing to be an old lady with Marianne, the two of us doing crazy things when our hair turns gray. It will be us one day, taking younger, cautious girls under our wings while we plan out how to make the most gruesome Halloween exhibits.

I am not ready to die like this. Not when my dreams of opening up a cupcake shop are finally coming true.

But Heather is simply stronger than me. No matter how hard I try, I cannot loosen her grip from my throat. My vision darkens around the edges, adding to my panic.

Heather's malicious face shouldn't be the last thing I see before I die. I want to see Marianne. Or Aunt Winnie.

When Karen's countenance floats in my vision, I decide her pretty face will do.

"Enough!" I hear Karen shout, and something dark flies in my periphery.

There is a loud bang, and miraculously, Heather's hands fall away from my throat.

Air so sweet I never knew I'd been underappreciating it all my life floods my lungs while I caress my throat. I try to clumsily scrub the feel of Heather's hands off my skin as I fall to my knees.

I blink as the world comes back into full view. The black around the edges of my vision are chased away by an image of true beauty: Karen is standing over Heather's limp body, clutching in her dainty fist the skillet Agnes used to make us all eggs for breakfast.

Karen's chest moves in and out unevenly, but she keeps her grip on the skillet, in case Heather rouses. "It's alright, Charlotte the Brave. Karen the Formidable won't let you fall."

My heart swells with love for Karen, erasing the sting of the hot coffee that's burned my skin. My relief is so acute that I barely register the ache from being choked nearly to death.

I guess that's the thing about true friends: no matter how dire life becomes, they will not leave you to fight your battles alone.

23

HALLOWEEN IN SWEETWATER FALLS

*W*hatever I was expecting the Halloween festival to be, I severely underestimated the work the people of Sweetwater Falls put into their individual exhibits. Though I am not generally a person for public displays of affection, when the fifth blood-soaked zombie pops out at me, I feel little shame in clinging to Logan's arm.

Of course, he has zero problem with this. Ever since Heather's arrest, Marianne and Logan have been taking turns sleeping on my couch, making sure I have everything I need.

Though Karen didn't sustain any injuries, we all insisted someone be with her for the next week until everyone's insides are a little less jumpy. Of course, when that was proposed, I didn't realize it would be subjecting me to the same treatment. Agnes has moved in with Karen since the attack, and Logan and Marianne have taken turns residing with Aunt Winnie and me.

I love our little unit, even more now that Logan has seamlessly slipped into the mix.

"Should we sit down for a minute?" Logan suggests, pausing before we get to the next booth. "Your heart is racing."

I twine my fingers through his. "I'm alright. I think the point of these things is to get your heart racing. It would be an insult if I showed up all calm and collected."

Logan kisses my temple, warming my insides with the softness of his lips. "Fair enough. What did you think of the last booth? We have to vote, you know." He narrows one eye at me. "Unbiased voting. Meaning you can't like the Live Forever Club's booth best before you've even seen it."

"Karen saved my life," I remind him. "Whatever she's doing, it's my new favorite."

Logan chuckles, keeping me close. "Fair enough." He watches the people in line in front of us step behind the curtain of the next exhibit. Each entry is about fifteen feet long by ten feet deep. I didn't think that would be enough space to really deliver a good scare, but I have been quite unpleasantly surprised by a few.

"The one with the zombies eating the spurting brains was disgusting. I wonder how many gallons of fake blood they'll go through by the time the festival is over."

Logan nods. "The high school kids really give it their all. There's got to be someone to keep the Live Forever Club on their toes. Competition is good for events like this. Every year, the production value gets better and better."

I wince when the people in front of us scream the second they go into Winifred's, Agnes' and Karen's booth. "I was really hoping one of these booths would be filled with like, carved pumpkins and candy apples."

Logan's nose crinkles. "You mean like, scary pumpkins?"

"No, like happy pumpkins. My version of Halloween is slightly more G-rated than this." I motion around the festival. Though, to be fair, a small bit of contentment and even a smidgen of joy rises in my chest when I take in the giggling people all around us. "I have to admit, this is fun. And everyone seems so happy to be scared. I like these events. Everyone getting together, trying something new. I like meeting new people and running into neighbors I didn't realize I'd been missing. Did you see Henry back there?"

"I sure did. He doesn't make a booth for the competition; he always dresses up like a skeleton scarecrow and walks around handing out pumpkin-shaped lollipops to the kids." Logan points to a person dressed in a giant pumpkin costume. "There's Dwight. He's got one of those mascot getups for every occasion. Last year he was a pumpkin with blood dripping out of the carved mouth."

"Charming."

Logan scratches the side of his face. "I guess in light of the recent town drama, he's opted for a regular pumpkin without the gore."

I motion toward Pumpkin Dwight, who stops to dance a jig for a few children. "But see? I love that this happens, even if it's a bit scary for me. I love the idea of a town coming together just to be together."

Sally flags me down, waving at me as she approaches with a candied apple on a stick in her hand. "Hi, honey. I'm glad to see you at a town event. I heard what happened." She shakes her head. "Just horrible."

I really don't want to talk about being almost poisoned by Heather and getting punched in the face. I really, really don't want to talk about nearly being choked to death.

I offer Sally a smile and point over to the portion of the apple cider booth marked clearly for adults. There, two middle-aged women are cheerfully taking tickets in exchange for cups of the Live Forever Club's special cider. "Good to see you, Sally. I bought you a cup of the Live Forever Club's wink-wink cider, as promised. It's being held for you over there at the booth. Thought you could use a little cheer. Toast to Judy?"

Sally's hand flutters to her chest, looking truly touched that I thought of her. "Thank you, sweetie. I think I will have a cup if it's to toast Judy." She points to the booth that we are next in line to walk into. "That one's a doosie. Might want to hold her extra tight, Logan," Sally says with a wink.

Logan holds onto my hand while I blush. "I think I can manage that." When Sally trots off, Logan elbows my side lightly. "You realize that you're one of us now, right? Next year, I vote you and I register and make our own booth. I bet ours will be the scariest of all."

My face lights up as I bob on the balls of my feet. "Oh! Can we do that? Can we get a booth, and inside, I'll just have my happy, sweet Halloween decorations? We won't win, but think of how confused everyone will be when they walk inside, expecting blood and guts."

The corner of Logan's mouth pulls up. "It's a date. Next year, it's you and me and fifty happy pumpkins."

Even though it's our turn to enter the Live Forever Club's booth, my feet still. We just made long-term plans. However silly they might be, that feels like a big step.

And I'm about to go into a booth designed to scare the sweetness out of me.

I chant over and over in my mind that this is just fun. This isn't real. Nothing in here is dangerous.

But all my mental preparation is for nothing when I step into the darkened booth. It is lit only by dim bulbs that flicker as if there is a problem with the wiring. An ominous creaking sound vibrates through my body, tuning me in to the show the ladies have spent the last month preparing.

Horror over seeing anything bad happen to my sweet aunt is amplified when she steps into the light with a jerk of her body.

Her hand rakes across her abdomen, causing her guts to spill out onto the floor in a bloody pile of gore.

I scream, unable to catch my breath before Agnes is rolled into the flickering light in a wheelbarrow, lying limp with a groan until an axe swings from out of nowhere. It severs her head off her shoulders, leaving it to land with a sickening plop on the floor.

I know it's papier-mâché. I remember Agnes talking about working with papier-mâché the night we had our slumber party, but I didn't realize she was making a replica of her own head. In the flickering light, it looks so real.

My stomach roils, not just because of the gore, but also because I cannot handle anything bad happening to that saint of a woman.

I turn to leave, but shriek when a rocking chair sounds behind us. I was so focused on the platform where the show was happening that I didn't think to check behind us. The black curtain apparently has a false backing, because it pulls open, still shrouded from the outside world, revealing Karen on a rocking chair.

With emotionless eyes she knits in her chair, rocking back and forth while she cackles, opening her mouth wide to display a cavernous jaw with no dentures. The light flickers on her while she laughs, chilling my bones far worse than anything I have witnessed thus far.

I don't know how they rigged it, but something that looks like a bat flies out of her mouth and darts across to the other side of the booth.

Even Logan shouts his horror at that.

We charge out of the booth, our chests heaving as we stare at each other with sheer fright plain on our faces. "I had no idea they were working on *that* all month!" I screech.

Logan laughs, his eyes wide as he clutches his chest, clearly winded. "That's the best one yet. Did you see that bat fly out of Karen's mouth?"

I shudder, grateful to be out of there. "I think I've had enough scares for one night. Maybe for the entire month, or even the year. Tomorrow night is all about passing out candy to little kids and making sure Karen's dentures never come out of her mouth again. That was terrifying!"

Marianne bounds up to us, throwing her arms around me. "Hey, you! Have you had a chance to try the apple cider? I swear, every time I finish a sip, I crave more. I've gone through three cups, and I still want another. Carlos is convinced I have a second stomach."

I politely decline, though a nice glass of apple cider sounds divine. "I'm good for now. Maybe we can bob for apples over there?" I point to a booth near the other side of the town square.

I'm not ready to drink something someone else hands me. The fact that I was a sip away from being poisoned by Heather still haunts me.

Logan seems to understand this. "How about I get you a bottled water instead?"

I nod, grateful he gets how mixed up I still sometimes feel about Heather's attack and subsequent arrest. Though it's been a week, and my burns from the coffee have healed, the puffiness of my cheek from where Heather bruised it still needs to be covered over with makeup.

Though, there are plenty of people in gory and gruesome costumes milling about, so perhaps I could have passed the black eye off as part of a Halloween getup.

I don't need to be thinking about almost being poisoned just because someone offers me a drink. Still, I haven't been able to shake the memory of Heather so possessed by her own insanity.

The arrest happened quickly, after Karen hit Heather over the head with the skillet and knocked her out. I can still picture Karen standing over Heather's limp form, pan in hand while we waited with shaky breath for Logan to show up with reinforcements.

Heather confessed to it all the moment the police came into the house with handcuffs. She murdered Judy for skimming tips. She broke into Judy's house to try to find loose cash. Then she poisoned Bill because he wouldn't give her time off.

Heather never made it to her music festival. She will end up spending the next chunk of her young life in jail for what she did to Judy and Bill.

Speaking of whom...

"Charlotte, glad I caught you." Bill calls to me, waving me over.

Though I haven't been anywhere without Logan or Marianne in a week, I take a chance and leave our circle to greet my former boss.

"Bill, I'm so glad you're on your feet. Are you sure you're feeling well enough to be here?"

Bill waves off my concern. "I'm alright now, thanks to you. The doctor told me that if I hadn't made it to the hospital when I did, I might not have made it at all." He lowers his chin as if readying to admit to a dirty crime. "Thanks for that."

I manage a small smile for the gruff man who treats gratitude like it needs a lowered voice and no witnesses for it to surface. "I'm just happy you're okay. I'm so sorry that happened to you. Is there anything I can do?"

The second my words hit the air, I regret them.

"As a matter of fact, there is. I was hoping to open tomorrow. I could use a waitress. I managed to hire someone to replace you, but maybe you could give me the day or two you had left of your two weeks and train them for me?"

I fight my childish nature, so my internal groan doesn't turn audible by mistake. "Sure, Bill. I can do that. No problem. You're really opening so soon?"

"People love my food. What can I say?"

I chew on my tongue to keep my snarky, "I really don't think that's why," from coming out. "I'll see you tomorrow, Bill."

When I turn to make my way back to Logan and Marianne, my gaze snags on Delia laughing a little too loudly at something Frank said that must have been hilarious. He still doesn't know that Delia is wise to his crush. I wonder if either of them will work up the courage to make the first move.

I wouldn't mind seeing companionship blooming into romance as autumn turns to winter.

I can't wait to see what this town has in store for Christmas.

When I hear the announcement that the donut on a string contest is about to commence, Marianne, Carlos, Logan and I jog excitedly over to the lineup, which consists mostly of kids, teens and men. Yet Marianne in all her daintiness fixes her face on her donut with sheer determination.

I rub her shoulders like I am prepping her to step into a boxing ring. "You know what to do, right? Remember your training. You've got this."

Marianne's jaw firms. "I can't believe the library lost to the post office for scariest building. I'm not going to lose this, too."

Marianne steps in with the line of competitors, who are all standing with their hands behind their backs, their faces mere inches from the string of spaced-out donuts.

Rip, the town selectman, stands atop a box with a megaphone in his hand, his belly pooched over his pants. "If everyone is ready, then help me count down. Five! Four!"

Carlos, Logan and I shout along until the bell rings, and everyone attacks their donuts.

It's fascinating to watch how many donuts drop to the ground (an immediate disqualification) within the first ten seconds. But Marianne is ready. She is prepared, determination fixed on her face. Her bites are aggressive while her tongue keeps the donut from falling to the grass. Her head twists and turns to accommodate the ring when there are only a few nibbles left.

I don't realize that I am jumping up and down with glee until Marianne is announced as the winner.

Carlos, Logan and I lead the way in obnoxious cheering, hooting and hollering without shame to celebrate a victory well won.

Marianne is beaming, her face smeared with sugar and cinnamon as Rip hoists her fist above her head.

She waxed poetic about Rip's speech he delivers about the winner of this event every year, so I am eager to hear it.

Rip's voice was built for announcing things, whether or not his words are paired with a megaphone. As his announcement carries through the festival, happiness bubbles in my chest that Marianne is receiving the accolade she has been craving for the past year.

"The winner this year is our Head Librarian, who used her vast vocabulary and book knowledge to defeat her foes. Every year, I am surprised by who rises to first place. Let no one look away from the face of triumph. Everyone shall voice their amazement and pride that our very own Marianne Magnolian has risen to the top spot in all the land." Rip turns into a poet, comparing the perfect circular shape of the dessert to the town of Sweetwater Falls, mentioning the love that never ends inside these city limits. Then Rip turns toward the table behind him, motioning to a giant donut on a tilted platter. The dessert is massive, stretching at least two feet in diameter. "And now, let the victor claim her trophy, declaring to all in Sweetwater Falls that there is no greater donut slayer than Marianne."

I cheer as loud as I can, happy to hear that everyone else is rejoicing as well. It is a tradition based on sugar and silliness, to be sure, but when Marianne claims her prize, posing for a picture with the huge donut they place in a golden box for her, I am so moved that a tear comes to my eye.

She did it. She really did it.

Marianne is a good person. She should have whatever she wants. If the thing she craves is a giant donut, then that's exactly what should happen.

Rip catches my eye and holds up his finger, making his way over to me. I don't know much about the man, other than his title, but he shakes my hand vigorously, his face pink. "Charlotte McKay. The new girl. I have to tell you, my wife placed an order for a dozen of your Halloween cupcakes, and boy, were we surprised! If only there was a contest for the scariest dessert. That would surely have won. Maybe next year."

I beam at the praise. "Thank you, sir. I had so much fun making them."

He grips Logan's shoulder and grins at Carlos. "Did you see what she did? She made pumpkin spice latte cupcakes and put edible crickets atop the cream cheese frosting. Nearly had a heart attack when I opened the box. Genius!"

Carlos shakes his head, blanching through his smile. "Did you eat the crickets?"

Rip claps Carlos on the back. "Would have been an insult not to. When someone goes all out, respect should be paid. Well done, young lady." Rip turns his head when someone calls his name near the donut tent. "If you'll excuse me. Duty calls."

He makes his way back to the cluster of people all recounting what a fantastic job Marianne did eating her donut without letting it fall.

I love how broad her smile is, how proud she is of this accomplishment. I could not love her more if I tried.

Logan twines his fingers through mine while we watch Marianne pose for pictures to be posted in the local paper, giving her statement of how she conquered this great feat to the reporter.

"I love that this is the sort of thing that makes the news," I muse to Logan.

"Oh, yes. They still cover the more unsavory events that take place, but the front page is always dedicated to something happy, like this. So, unless a three-legged puppy suddenly gets fitted with a wheelchair, Marianne might just make the front page of the news when it rolls out next week."

I can't stop bobbing on the balls of my feet. Even as Marianne finishes up and stores her giant donut prize behind the table, my joy cannot be quelled.

When she greets Carlos with a gleeful hug, he lifts her off the ground and spins her in the air, unleashing her giggles so that they spill all over the citizens of Sweetwater Falls. He sets her down with a precious kiss to her nose.

"I'm so proud of you!" I tell Marianne as I throw my arms around her neck, squeezing a squeak out of her.

"I'm kind of proud of me, too!" Marianne squeaks. "I did it! I can't believe I actually did it!"

Logan points toward a corner booth. "Can I buy the champion, her gentleman friend and her best friend a cup of Tom's Halloween stew?"

Marianne tilts her nose in the air, as if she is true royalty. "You may."

I love everything about my life in Sweetwater Falls. I link one arm through Marianne's and the other through Logan's, casting a grin at Carlos. We make our way through the sea of gleeful faces. We shake Pumpkin Dwight's hand and even pose for a picture with him in his enormous orange suit. I greet at least two dozen people by name because that is what you do in your hometown.

Though Sweetwater Falls has its quirks peppered with a few

dismal moments, I am always grateful that fate brought me here —to my family, to my friends, and to the possibility of cupcakes.

The End

Love the book?
Leave a review!

PUMPKIN SPICE LATTE CUPCAKES

Yield: 24 Cupcakes

From the cozy mystery novel *Pumpkin Spice Scare*
by Molly Maple

*"I can do a yellow cake with pumpkin spice. That's usually cloves,
nutmeg, cinnamon and ginger. Sometimes allspice. It smells better
than a pumpkin pie and tastes like a hug."*

-*Pumpkin Spice Scare*

Ingredients for the Cupcake:
   2/3 cup unsalted butter, softened
   1¾ cup granulated sugar
   2 large eggs, room temperature
   2 tsp pure vanilla extract
   2½ cups all-purpose flour
   1½ tsp baking powder
   ½ tsp salt
   1 cup whole milk

1 tsp instant coffee
1 tsp ground cinnamon
½ tsp ground ginger
½ tsp allspice
¼ tsp ground nutmeg
1/8 tsp ground cloves

Instructions for the Cupcake:

1. Preheat the oven to 350°F and line a cupcake pan with cupcake liners.
2. In a medium bowl, sift together 2½ cups flour, 1½ tsp baking powder, ½ tsp salt, 1 tsp ground cinnamon, ½ tsp ground ginger, ½ tsp allspice, ¼ tsp ground nutmeg, 1/8 tsp ground cloves. Set flour mixture aside.
3. In a large bowl, use a mixer to beat the butter and sugar on medium speed for three minutes. Beat until shiny, scraping down the sides of the bowl as needed.
4. Add eggs one at a time while the mixer runs on low speed. Add 1 tsp pure vanilla extract. Mix until smooth.
5. Dissolve 1 tsp of instant coffee into 1 cup of whole milk.
6. With the mixer on low speed, add the flour mixture in thirds, alternating with the coffee milk. Mix to incorporate with each addition, scraping down the sides of the bowl as needed. Beat until just combined.
7. Divide the batter into your lined cupcake pan, filling each one 2/3 the way full.
8. Bake for 17-20 minutes at 350°F, or until a toothpick stuck in the center comes out clean.

Ingredients for the Pumpkin Cream Cheese Frosting:

8 oz (1 package) cream cheese, softened

¼ cup unsalted butter, softened

¼ cup canned pumpkin

4 cups powdered sugar

1 tsp pure vanilla extract

1 ½ tsp ground cinnamon

½ tsp ground ginger

½ tsp ground nutmeg

24 edible crickets

Instructions for the Frosting:

1. Beat the cream cheese, butter and pumpkin in a large bowl until well-combined and fluffy.
2. Add the powdered sugar, one cup at a time, beating on low speed. Scrape down the sides of the bowl often.
3. Add vanilla extract, cinnamon, ground ginger and nutmeg. Beat until shiny and smooth.
4. Spread over cooled cupcakes. Top with an edible cricket.

UNTITLED

Enjoy a free preview of *Peppermint Peril*,
book five in the Cupcake Crimes series.

Peppermint Peril

PEPPERMINT PERIL PREVIEW

CHAPTER ONE

I have never been more stressed in my life. Or if I have, I cannot recall it, nor do I want to relive anything close to the anxiety that causes this pounding in my chest. Sweat runs down my spine as I pick up the box of cupcakes, praying none of them tipped or tilted on the drive. I was so careful, going well below the meager speed limit and taking each turn with care as if I were transporting an unbuckled newborn.

This is why I make people pick up their cupcakes. The Bravery Bakery has been my sole source of income for almost a month now. Generally, I feel like I've got the hang of things, except when Nick and Nancy asked if they could pay extra for me to deliver their order. I said yes without thinking of how stressful it is to drive baked goods from one home to another.

"It's going to be fine," Marianne tells me from her spot in the passenger seat of my red sedan. "Not one person has complained that when they took their cupcakes home, everything was smashed to pieces."

All I take out of my best friend's assurance is the visual of my hours of hard work being smashed to pieces inside the delivery boxes.

Marianne grimaces. "That was supposed to make you feel better, but I think you just turned paler."

"This is my first catering job. If I screw this up, it will be my only catering job."

Marianne runs her fingers through her chin-length chestnut hair. She turns her head so the meager winter sun can shine on her olive skin through the window. "I'm right here, Charlotte McKay. Nothing bad is going to happen to those desserts."

I park the car in front of Nick and Nancy's sizable colonial, gaping at the pretty white shutters set against the stately brick. Leading up to the house are a dozen small, well-trimmed bushes shaped to look like Christmas trees, complete with blue and white twinkling lights. There are candles in every window, and an enormous Christmas wreath at the front door.

Though the white-haired couple seemed sweet and unassuming when they booked the job with me, I can see they have expensive taste and put thought into the details.

My stomach sinks. "Oh my goodness. I put sprinkles on the peppermint cupcakes."

Marianne tilts her head at me. "Red and green sprinkles. What's wrong with that? I think they're cute."

I shake my head with plenty of self-loathing flooding my system, suddenly regretting my choices that seemed fitting at the time. "No, no, no. It's all wrong. They like things expensive and upscale. Red and green sprinkles are fun and festive. My design is all wrong." I pinch the bridge of my nose. "It's going to look cheap against the backdrop of all this." I motion to the perfect house that looks like it should be featured on a Christmas card.

Marianne reaches across the console and squeezes my hand. "You're freaking out. It's going to be just fine. Nick and Nancy are fun people. Nick plays Santa Claus at the Christmas Festival every year, and Nancy is Mrs. Claus. Don't let the house fool you; they're giant sweetheart goofballs."

I lean my head against the back of my seat. "We are never catering again. This is so stressful. I'm going to ruin their party."

I don't expect Marianne to chuckle at me, but the sound adds a little levity to my certain doom. "If cupcakes can make or break a party, then it's a pretty boring affair, isn't it. Let's go, Charlotte. You'll see there's nothing to worry about."

I take my time getting out of the car, steeling myself for the worst-case scenario.

The cupcakes are smashed to pieces.

The cookies have crumbled.

The donuts have staled and cracked.

I suck in a deep breath when I open my trunk, hoping I haven't screwed up my first catering gig. I pop open the lid of the box, heaving a sigh of relief when I see none of the cupcakes have tilted.

Marianne grabs up two boxes of desserts, scolding me with a light tease. "You are going to give yourself an ulcer, worrying like this. Desserts are fun. Enjoy the ride, Charlotte the Brave. You've got this."

Without Marianne, I would be nothing close to calm.

When I ring the doorbell and am greeted by Nancy, relief floods my features.

The little woman with pinned white hair and minimal makeup is dressed as Mrs. Claus, complete with an apron lined with candy canes. She lights up at the sight of us. "Oh, perfect timing! I told everyone the dinner started at five o'clock, but half of my guests decided to show up an hour early to mingle. They've gone through most of my hors d'oeuvres and dinner is nowhere near ready. They can snack on your cookies while we wait for the rest of the guests to arrive."

Marianne kisses Nancy on the cheek. "Where would you like us to set the desserts, Mrs. Claus?"

"Follow me, girls." She ushers us into the house and leads us past the giant Christmas tree in the foyer, around the even bigger Christmas tree in the living room, and toward a grand table laden with picked-over trays in the dining room. "Can you put the donuts and cookies here for people to eat now? We'll save the cupcakes for after dinner." She motions to a silver tray in the center. "You can use that to set them on. It's almost time for the party to start." Her doorbell rings. "Excuse me!"

"Of course," I reply, my throat dry. Christmas music plays in the background, highlighting the season amid the garland and nutcrackers everywhere I look.

The doorbell rings, and Nancy throws her hands up, pleasantly exasperated. "The hostess' work is never done, it seems. Thank goodness you took over desserts this year, Charlotte. I honestly don't know what I would have done. Every year, our Christmas party gets bigger and bigger. Last year, it was thirty people. This year we are expecting fifty!" She wrings her hands as she makes her way out of the dining room. "Oh, I hope I made enough ham."

Marianne and I share a "yikes" look between us. We begin popping open the lids on our boxes so we can fill the giant silver tray with donuts and cookies.

The cookies haven't crumbled, and the donuts haven't staled. I laugh to myself at how stressed I was over nothing.

"You make the desserts look all pretty on the tray," Marianne instructs. "I'm going to consolidate some of these hors d'oeuvres, so it doesn't look as picked over. Sheesh, people showed up early, and her appetizers are halfway gone before the party's even started."

We work quickly and in tandem, no doubt because we have spent so much time together in the kitchen, baking and laughing in a happy rhythm while we work to make my dream of owning my own cupcakery come true.

By the time the donuts and cookies are set up, Marianne is

finished making the hors d'oeuvres look fresh and well-presented. She gathers up the unused trays and I take the boxes of cupcakes, following her to the kitchen.

Everything smells like ham and butter. My mouth waters because it is not possible to remain unaffected when an aroma this enticing enters your nose. All that is needed to complete the picture of perfection is a roaring fireplace and a plateful of cookies.

"Now don't you feel silly, worrying like you did? Nancy is a sweetheart, and your cupcakes are amazing. Christmas is all about red and green, which you did with the sprinkles."

I smile at her as I set the cupcake boxes on the counter. All the worry is leaving me, taking weight off my spine and shoulders so I stand taller, embracing every centimeter of my five-foot-ten inches. "You're right. Next time I start spiraling, I'll try to remember how much I stressed out today, and how it was all for nothing." I cast around the immaculate kitchen. "Any guesses where a clean tray might be for me to set the cupcakes out for her?"

Marianne shrugs. "Check the cupboards." She motions around the kitchen. "And for the record, my kitchen looks nothing like this when I cook for a party. Hers is perfectly clean. Mine generally looks like a culinary bomb went off if I try cooking a huge feast." She shakes her head. "I suspect Nick and Nancy actually have Christmas elves working around the house for them, cleaning when no one is looking."

I chuckle at Marianne's positing. "It's the only explanation."

She stands over the stove and inhales deeply, her eyes rolling back. "I'm warning you, if we don't get set up and get out of here soon, I'm going to open up that oven and start picking at the ham. It smells too delicious to resist."

Marianne sets the dirty trays in the dishwasher while I open cupboards to see if I can locate something on which I can display my cupcakes.

"Agreed. Eating my weight in ham all I can think about right now. My parents and I never did big meals like that around Christmas," I tell Marianne. "We usually just got takeout."

Marianne's nose crinkles. "No offense to your childhood, but that is not happening this year. You live with Winifred now. If there's anything your great-aunt is good at, it's making a killer Christmas dinner. The Live Forever Club's cooking skills really shine around the holidays. Agnes makes the potatoes with so much butter, I could eat only that and be totally satisfied. Karen makes wassail and usually a few side dishes—again with enough butter to stop a horse's heart. Winifred makes ham with pineapples." Marianne swoons, shutting the dishwasher door. "It's heavenly."

I have no idea what wassail is, but everything else sounds delicious. "What do you make?"

"A mess, usually." Marianne chuckles at herself. "I bring a salad. It's hard to mess that up. Our Christmas dinner is always on Christmas Eve—the day after the town's big Christmas Festival. That's a whole thing of its own. You'll love it."

"I've loved every event I've been to in Sweetwater Falls so far, so I have no doubt the Christmas Festival will be just as fun." I tug open the last cupboard, my mouth pulling to the side when I find nothing larger than a dinner plate, which won't do. "There has been so much going on lately; it will be nice to relax a little and enjoy the holidays. I'm looking forward to a peaceful, calm season. I'm not working at the diner anymore, so I don't have the stress of working two jobs. The Bravery Bakery is going well, thanks to my beautiful baking assistant."

Marianne takes a bow. She's making light of the praise she is due, but I mean it sincerely. Without her coming over after her shifts at the library a couple times a week, I would never have been able to open the bakery, and I certainly wouldn't be where I am today. Expanding my business to include catering parties wasn't in the business plan, but when I told Marianne about Nick and Nancy's request, she pushed me to accept the job, telling me it was too early in the game to start limiting my business.

She was right, as usual.

I tuck a stray blonde curl back into my bun, frowning at my best friend. "I'm not sure what to put the cupcakes on," I admit to Marianne as Nick strolls into the kitchen. "Hi, Nick. Lovely house you have here. And the decorations are spectacular. How long did all of this take you?"

Nick is dressed as an off-duty Santa Claus. He is clad in dress pants with a red suit jacket over his crisp white collared shirt covering his bulbous belly. His white beard is neatly trimmed in an arc two inches from his chin. His white hair is combed neatly, curling at his neck. He's even got that jolly twinkle in his eye that makes you want to promise you've been very good this year, so he brings you a new doll.

He opens the oven and peeks at the ham. "Oh, we start decorating around Halloween. It takes a fair bit of time to get it all just right. And we keep adding to the collection every year, so it gets a little more lavish each season. Did you see the array of nutcrackers? I started collecting them when I came home from the war, and never stopped. I'd like to say I only buy one a year, but that would make me easily two hundred years old." He chortles and closes the oven door. "Thanks for taking over the desserts this year, girls. I can actually greet my guests, and Nancy wasn't up all night baking. Quite the luxury."

"It's no trouble." I pop open one of the cupcake boxes. "You don't happen to have a tray, do you? Something we can set our cupcakes on."

Nick motions to the pantry. "Top shelf." The doorbell rings

again, bringing a laugh from the man. "A host's duty is never done. The party doesn't start until five o'clock, but our first guest arrived before four." He checks his watch. "I guess the party has officially started now. A bunch of people just got here."

Marianne shakes her head with a smile. "Who came an hour early?"

Nick bats his hand as if to excuse his mild complaining. "Delia. She likes to look at all the nutcrackers, see if she can spot the new ones."

Delia is known to be the town gossip, but I didn't realize she was so fascinated with nutcrackers. I personally think the things are a tad creepy, but to each their own, I guess. Though, I can see the appeal of coming early to scope out the massive amounts of decorations. It takes time to absorb it all.

I throw open the pantry door, hoping to find the perfect tray (or at this point, any clean tray).

I shriek when a person tumbles out at me. Someone must have been propped up against the closed door on the inside of the pantry, because the second I open it, the man falls onto me, knocking me over and pinning me to the tiled floor.

Marianne bleats her distress as she darts over to us. "Oh! Charlotte, are you okay?"

I have no idea how to make heads or tails of the heavy body atop me until Marianne helps me roll the man off me, splaying him on the floor to my left. Marianne helps me up, brushing me off while I shudder, confused and thoroughly frightened that someone fell asleep inside the pantry, standing up.

I drop to my knees beside the man, feeling for a pulse when slamming down atop me didn't appear to wake him.

Marianne covers her mouth with her hand, stuffing in a cry of anguish when it becomes clear that this man is not going to be getting up ever again.

My scream slices through the merriment of the Christmas music, bringing several people to the kitchen.

Worried cries splinter out through the home when the scene unfolds to the partygoers. "What did you do?" someone asks in horror. "Is that Tom? Oh, no!"

It is then I realize that I am kneeling beside a dead body, looking very much like the killer smack in the middle of Santa Claus' kitchen.

Read *Peppermint Peril* today!

ABOUT THE AUTHOR

Author Molly Maple believes in the magic of hot tea and the romance of rainy days.

She is a fan of all desserts, but cupcakes have a special place in her heart. Molly spends her days searching for fresh air, and her evenings reading in front of a fireplace.

Molly Maple is a pen name for USA Today bestselling fantasy author Mary E. Twomey, and contemporary romance author Tuesday Embers.

Visit her online at www.MollyMapleMysteries.com. Sign up for her newsletter to be alerted when her next new release is coming.

Made in the USA
Las Vegas, NV
10 January 2022

41060987R00104